ANSWERING FIRE

BOOKS BY JOHN WHEATCROFT

Poetry
Death of a Clown
Prodigal Son
A Voice from the Hump
Gowpen: A Double Handful of Poems, with Karl Patten (limited
    edition)
Declaring Generations, with Peter Balakian (limited edition)
Ordering Demons
The Stare on the Donkey's Face
Random Necessities

Fiction
Edie Tells
Catherine, Her Book
The Beholder's Eye
Killer Swan
Mother of All Loves
Trio with Four Players
The Education of Malcolm Palmer
Slow Exposures (stories)

Drama
Ofoti
*A Fourteenth Century Poet's Vision of Christ: A Poetic Drama for
    Voices and Instruments* (music by Thomas Beversdorf)

Interviews
Our Other Voices: Nine Poets Speaking (edited by John Wheatcroft)

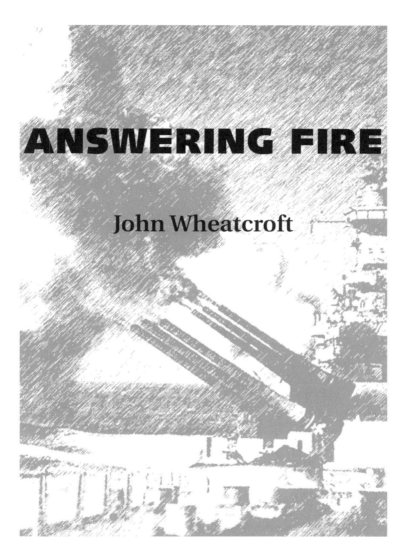

ANSWERING FIRE

John Wheatcroft

Lunar Offensive Press

1910 Foster Avenue
Brooklyn NY 11230-1902

"irrevovcable as flesh,
the gazing eye
falls through the world"
Ono no Komachi
tr. Kennneth Rexroth

Cover Photo "Nine-Gun Salvo," by Dom Menta
January 19, 1955

Author Photo by Terry Wild

Other photos US Navy

The author and publisher express heartfelt thanks to Dom Menta, webmaster
and the USS Wisconsin Association
http://www.usswisconsin.org/
for invaluable assistance in the preparation of graphics for this book.

Thanks to Alan Gold.

Production by Joel Cohen, Ragged Edge Press, NYC

ISBN 0-976-5611-1-5

to Thomas Yoseloff

Lest thou forget the things which thine eyes have seen.

—Deuteronomy 4:9

CONTENTS

Acknowledgments • **xi**

Kamikaze • 1

Answering Fire • 25

ACKNOWLEDGMENTS

The author acknowledges Cornwall Books and Thomas Yoseloff, Ltd., for permission to make use of passages, most of which have been slightly altered, from poems of his that appear in *Prodigal Son, Ordering Demons,* and *Random Necessities,* and for permission to reprint the story "Kamikaze," which appears in *Slow Exposures.*

The author is grateful to Steve Fried for the commitment he has made to this publication by devoting energy, expertise and wisdom.

KAMIKAZE

THEN THE KAMIKAZES CAME AND EVERY MAN ABOARD felt it. As though something inside were inflating him. Like the bladder of a football. And no way to release the pressure. Soon it would explode. Right through his skin.

Of course it shows. A way of standing comes over a man. Feet astride, flat against the deck. Arms folded across the chest or hanging at the sides, not loose but slightly bent, the veins of the forearms showing tight, like halyards lashed against a big blow. Hands halfway into fists.

And a look comes over a man. There's a way the jaw has of clamping against the top teeth. A way of holding the mouth— as though a bitter bite that can't be swallowed or spit out sits on the tongue. Instead of sliding back and forth across their sockets, the eyes jerk from here to there. When they rest, they tear through the surface of things and bore on in.

All of them could feel it growing, like a runaway tumor. They sensed it in everybody else too. All of a sudden a man would find himself just standing waiting for it. From down in the powder chamber at the bottom of each of the turrets. When it came, it would rip through the sixteen-plate steel. Cracking the armored hull as though it were an eggshell.

Imagine what it does to the living together—to whatever lies between this one and that of the three thousand bodies and souls jammed onto a floating wedge of steel. Scarcely a day passes without two men—they might be total strangers or the best of friends—starting for each other like a couple of musky rams. And when they're dragged apart and the lieutenant or the division petty officer asks them what it's about, they honestly don't know. Every morning there's another story about some seaman and a boatswain or some boatswain and a gunner's mate or some gunner's mate and one of the j.g.'s from communications.

That's how it was while the kamikazes were coming, before the typhoon. Then during the storm everything went unhinged without falling apart. Like a plaster-of-Paris doll dropped and broken but held together from inside by wires. And afterward, the great calm.

*   *   *

For over a week the sea had been smooth as the sky. During the day he could follow the wake of a flying fish hundreds of yards. At night the reflected light of the big-bellied moon and of the whole sweep of the stars turned the track of the ships of the task force into miles of silver-green furrows plowed across a flat dark field.

Days had gone by without a single plane diving on them from the sun or sneaking over the horizon and skimming at them low across the water. Not even flares or tinfoil at night to unnerve them and foul the radar screen. He could scarcely believe they were still fighting a war.

A midwatch. He sat on the starboard flagbag, almost doubting he was at sea. A sailor has a clinometer inside his gut—whatever the angle of the axis of his body, something always points straight up and down. This internal instrument told him there was no rolling, no pitching, not the least.

The big box-like carriers, riding high out of the water. The cruisers and the other battleship, the barrels of their main batteries, slightly elevated, pointing toward the horizon like accusing fingers. The destroyers beyond, skulking low in the water like sharks. All of them jet silhouettes against a green-black sky. Leaning all the way back on the tarpaulin covering the flags, Bond fixed his eye on the bulging moon.

Sometime after 0100, Fels, joe-man of the watch, showed up with two mugs of coffee. He handed one to Bond and stood sipping the other himself. To have him stay annoyed Bond—night watches were the only private time to be had. While trying to ignore him by ranging his eye back and forth across the great curve of the sky, Bond sensed that Fels was asking for his attention.

After a while, unable to hold out any longer, he glanced at Fels. Fels was very short, with a huge head and thick chest. His shoulders sloped sharply and his loose-hanging arms bent at elbow and wrist. Like a stunted bear. With his left foot hiked onto the edge of the flagbag, his back and head poker-straight, the coffee mug balanced on the upturned tips of his fingers, Fels seemed to be striking a pose. Suddenly it hit Bond—Fels was imitating Mappes. In spite of his irritation Bond couldn't help laughing.

As though the laugh were a signal, Fels started to twirl the mug on his fingertips, a habit of Mappes' which Bond was surprised the slow-witted Fels had taken note of. As the mug came around, Bond saw the red letters painted on the side—M.A.P.P.E.S. That Fels dared burlesque Mappes and drink from Mappes' own mug while Mappes slept below sent Bond into a second fit of laughter.

Then Fels looked right at Bond. Something about Fels' way of taking him in always made Bond uncomfortable. Fels' eyes seemed to fasten on Bond's lips. As if he were trying to discover how Bond pronounced his words. Another thing—Fels' mouth always hung open. He seemed to be struggling to hear through it, to want to drink in sounds and meanings.

Trying for more laughter, Fels leaned over and sucked a fat mouthful of coffee. Then throwing back his head he allowed the coffee to run slowly down his throat, savoring. Across his face lay the precise look of petty arrogance Mappes wore. Fels grinned at his own antic. Suddenly, with an explosive clearing of his throat, he spit. Bond heard the spit hit the side of the mug, saw it roll down across the two red P.'s, then onto Fels' fingers. Revolted as he was, Bond laughed for the third time.

Again the laugh triggered Fels. Leaping back from the flag-bag, he laid the wall of the mug in the palm of his right hand and cocked his arm toward the rail, threatening to throw. Then he turned to Bond and searched his face. The sneaky daring of Fels, the childlike display of his hatred for Mappes, the delight he took in revealing his feelings, these drew still more laughter from Bond. In the middle of the laugh Fels heaved Mappes' mug toward the sea.

Bond was stunned. In awful fascination his eye followed the spiraling mug through the greenness hanging between sky and water. Even from the height of the signal bridge, Bond could see the silver splash. He kept staring at the spot until the sea closed back. As he looked at Fels a vague horror caused him to shudder.

Fels erupted into a howl. The bellow of some jungle animal. As though his tongue, riveted flat to the bottom of his mouth, were unable to articulate sounds. As though the tongue were too big, the tongue of an ape in the mouth of a man. As Bond watched Fels wipe the spit from his knuckles onto the front of his chambray shirt, horror gave way to revulsion.

Afterward, while he sat alone on the flagbag, staring at the sea and picturing Mappes' mug sinking deeper and deeper into the blackness, the horror returned. With it came a tinge of pleasure, which caused his flesh to tingle. Like the first touch of a prostitute's fingers on his cheek. Even later in his bunk he couldn't erase the image of the drowning mug from his mind.

Sometime during the morning watch Mappes discovered his private mug was missing. At eight o'clock quarters he stormed and blustered and accused and threatened the division for a full fifteen minutes. While his eye probed the ranks for a plausible target, his voice ack-acked away—"Some gutless bastard broke it, then heaved it over the side." . . . "When I catch the sonuvabitch I'll string 'im to the yardarm by the toes." . . . "If somebody don't come clean they ain't gonna be no more joe for nobody." Olivio, joe-man for the second watch, Griffen, joe-man for the first, Mappes' own, and Fels, joe-man for the third, all disclaimed knowing anything. When Mappes' eye hit Bond as it ran down the second row, Bond was terrified by the secret knowledge he held.

During the next few days Mappes blistered their hands and knees with work and lashed their nerves raw with his tongue.

But he didn't make good his threat to secure the joe-gear. His own stomach so craved coffee that he satisfied his stomach before his pride. Ross, the most talented hand on the bridge, painted M.A.P.P.E.S. with red lead on a brand new mug Mappes procured from one of the cooks.

For withholding what, if revealed, would have eased the weight of Mappes on the entire division, Bond felt guiltier each day. He resolved to inform. But as soon as he closed on Mappes, he found his tongue locked. He also became aware of a kind of loyalty to Fels. A loyalty he did not want. It disgusted him.

Fels seemed unconcerned about the possibility of Bond's informing. When they met on the bridge or in the sleeping compartment or in the chow line, Fels gave no sign that anything lay between them. This both relieved and irritated Bond. He felt he deserved some acknowledgment for keeping silent. It came.

Another week behind them. Though the flame of his anger had pretty well burned out, Mappes was still smoldering. Secured from his day's work above, Bond had gone below and showered. He was climbing the ladder to the forecastle in order to go aft for the evening meal when the top of his eye picked up someone standing beside the hatch, waiting to descend. Fels. Quickly Bond glanced past him. Then because he sensed Fels staring after him, instead of going down the ladder, Bond looked back. On Fel's face lay a grin. An impudent, insinuating grin. "We're old friends," it said. "No need to pretend when we're alone. Let's own each other." The full resentment did not hit Bond until minutes later, as he stood in line above the mess compartment. The return of the image of the drowning mug caused him to forego coffee with his meal.

But he was handed a mug on the midwatch that night. When

Fels didn't turn and head for the shelter, Bond wasn't surprised. Again he leaned all the way back on the tarpaulin and studied the sky. Just a slice of the moon. He picked out both dippers and Orion, then located the pole star. In order to empty his mind he fixed on that one point of light. But he couldn't lose the sense of Fels standing close, pulling at his attention. Against his will he left the sky for Fels.

The same grin was there. Then Bond noticed the pair of semaphore sticks, cloth rolled tight, stuck through the beltloop of Fel's dungarees. Precisely the way Mappes carried his own flags. All at once Bond realized that they were not orange and yellow sailcloth, but Mappes' very flags—handsewn silk, crimson and gold. Fels swished the sticks from his beltloop with the flourish of a matinee idol unsheathing his sword, unfurling and separating the flags in the same motion. Then, belly sucked in, legs astride, he began a burlesque that caught the manner of Mappes so precisely that, in spite of himself, once more Bond broke into a laugh.

Encouraged, Fels went on, semaphoring faster and more furiously. He wasn't spelling out words. Bond wondered whether he could read and write; certainly he hadn't learned any of the shorthand of the signalman. But to Bond's surprise Fels was forming letters. The sight of the dull-witted Fels imitating Mappes to perfection by making symbols whose meaning he did not understand with Mappes' own flags soon had Bond roaring with laughter. And the more wildly Fels bent and unbent his arms, rolled and flailed the flags, the harder and louder Bond laughed.

Just when Bond found himself laughing so that tears ran out of his eyes, Fels jerked his arms to a stop directly over his head.

With childlike craft he grinned at Bond, then raised his eyes toward the flags. A second later he flung the sticks to the deck and began to stomp on the crimson and gold silk under his thick-soled shoes. Bond shivered. Suddenly Fels leaped back, then slowly reached down and picked up the flags. Carefully he twirled the cloth around the sticks, as he'd seen Mappes do hundreds of times. But instead of sliding Mappes' flags back into his beltloop, Fels chucked them end over end into the darkness. They hit the water silently. Bond, once again amazed and fascinated, horrified and excited, climbed from the flagbag and stood at the rail beside Fels. Together they watched the floating flags slowly diminish behind the ship. The crimson half was the last to disappear.

Mappes' performance at quarters next morning was something to behold. His fury was a visible force. Ramming his fist into his hand and spitting out curses without minding their meaning, he stomped up and down the deck. Every so often he thought of a man who might have a fresh grudge against him— someone he had recently dressed down, abused, punished, bullied, humiliated. Breaking through ranks he stormed up to the suspect until their mouths almost touched, and with fists pumping, the veins in his throat and temples bulging, Mappes ordered, dared, begged the man to admit he'd stolen the flags or thrown them overboard. A quarter of the men in the division took this sledgehammering. While Mappes was pounding Demaestri, directly behind Bond, Bond ventured a glance at Fels. In Fel's face, thick-featured, open-mouthed, vacant-eyed, lay a stupidity that protected more surely than the saintliest character or the sworn word of a hundred witnesses. As before, Bond was terrified by the secret knowledge he held. So enormous did Mappes make the crime that Bond felt that to shield or reveal Fels was a matter of life or death.

Mappes didn't forget his semaphore flags; he didn't let the men forget them. At sea silk flags couldn't be replaced. Although he took to wearing a regulation pair through his belt, it wasn't the same. There was no fine material, no rich color to mark off Mappes' flags from the six or eight G.I. pair on the bridge. Day after day Mappes bent their backs with still more hours of work. Each day they hated him more intensely.

Heavier than the work on Bond's back was the guilt he felt for not sparing the rest of his shipmates by exposing one. Especially because ironically Fels was the only man to escape Mappes' fury. The day Fels had reported aboard fresh from boot camp, Mappes had taken a look at his vacant eyes, hanging jaw, rock-like features and decided he was a special case. Instead of striking for his rate by learning to send and receive flashing light and semaphore, Fels served as permanent joe-man of the third watch. For cleaning station Mappes had assigned Fels the single-stool head inside the passageway behind the signal shelter. Mappes himself, sensing the appropriateness, had nicknamed Fels "Shithead." The dirt-stiff, food-stained, sweat-smelling dungarees Fels wore, his corroded, salt-white shoes, his frayed hat, yellow with soap and black from his head around the bottom rim, these perfectly fit the name. To every man in the division, all the petty officers, the chief, sometimes even the ensign and the lieutenant, he was Shithead Fels. As though "Shithead" were his given or baptismal name. Fels made no objection. He didn't even mind that as an adjective, adverb, noun, and verb his nickname became the most commonly used word on the bridge. To intensify in any direction a person, thing, action, quality, situation, all a man did was to interject a "Shithead."

Mappes' use of him as an orderly also set Fels apart. When he wanted cigarettes or razor blades or soap at the canteen, Mappes sent Fels to do his buying. When gedunk was sold in the aft messhall or small stores opened in the fantail, Mappes dispatched Fels to bring him back a sundae or a couple of tee shirts or pairs of skivvies. Twice a week Fels changed Mappes' mattress cover, and every Monday morning when "Air bedding" was piped, Fels hauled Mappes' mattress and blankets from the sleeping compartment and lashed them over the lifeline on the forecastle. Fels even shined Mappes' shoes. Just as he accepted his duties as permanent joe-man and head-cleaner, just as he answered to Shithead, Fels fagged for Mappes without the least objection.

In other ways Mappes treated Fels like a favorite son. Only Fels could arrive late for quarters without feeling the whip of Mappes' tongue. Only Fels dared sit against the bulkhead or lie napping on the deck during working hours without drawing three midwatches running or hours of extra duty. Only Fels could be caught asleep in the signal shelter during a midwatch without being thrown on report and facing a Saturday morning Captain's mast. While bearing down on the division to vent his rage and demonstrate his authority, Mappes made a constant point of exempting Fels. That squeezed Bond's bowels.

Returning from supper about a week after the semaphore flags went overboard, Bond found a large orange lying on his bunk. One of two pieces of fresh fruit doled out to each hand every seven days. Instantly Bond knew from whom it had come. Even while he sucked the orange greedily, he felt uneasy. He knew that by accepting the precious piece of fruit he was assenting to what he read in Fels' grin. Lying in his sack unable to sleep between lights out and midwatch, he wished with all his heart he hadn't eaten Fels' orange.

As he sat on the flagbag during the first hour of the watch, Bond was sure Fels would appear. There was almost no moon. Just a silver rim. He was very tired. Fearing he might fall asleep if he lay back on the tarpaulin, he sat forward, his face buried in his hands. All at once he sensed someone close by. Expecting to find Fels, Bond was startled to see the form of Mappes confronting him.

Mappes was in a characteristic pose—facing outboard, feet apart, belly sucked in—the long glass he kept in the shelter for his own use jammed against the eye. A surge of hatred made Bond's blood leap. On instinct he fisted his right hand. His eye darted to Mappes' right temple. Closing his eyes, in his imagination he was able to feel the wallop of his knuckles against Mappes' skull, to see Mappes crash sideward to the deck. Opening his eyes, Bond's arm went limp, his fingers fell unclenched. As his eyes re-focused in the silver grayness of the night, the figure of Mappes was transformed into Fels.

Partly from relief, partly from the comical idea of Fels staring at nothing on the midnight horizon through the long glass Mappes would allow no one but himself to use, Bond erupted into laughter. Fels dropped the glass from his eye and wrapped both of his hands around the eyepiece. Like a man at a carnival about to try his strength with a heavy wooden hammer, Fels lifted the long glass high over his head, then smashed it down on the two-plate steel shield beside the flagbag. The glass hit with a surprisingly soft ring. Near the middle the barrel bent, almost to a ninety degree angle. Fels grinned at the glass as it lay across the top of the shield, then at Bond. Less horrified than excited over what he knew was about to happen, Bond watched Fels seize the now boomerang-shaped glass, tuck it under his wrist, and twirling himself on the deck like a discus thrower, heave it end over end into the night. Again Bond and Fels watched the spot until the dark sea came smooth.

Bond expected Mappes to be beside himself with rage at quarters the next morning. He wasn't. He didn't even announce that the glass was missing. At first Bond thought Mappes hadn't noticed the empty rack. But remembering Mappes' ritual of hauling the glass from the shelter each morning as soon as the first misty light filtered over the horizon, then carefully sweeping the sea from both sides of the bridge, he considered it unlikely Mappes didn't know. While Mappes was running down the muster list, his voice seemed anything but belligerent. Bond looked at Mappes carefully. Instead of strutting up and down the ranks defiantly, his eyes seemed to be tiptoeing. Every now and then they darted back over his shoulder. At least a dozen times in the three or four minutes he held the men at quarters, Bond saw Mappes wipe the palm of his hand across his partly opened mouth. Like a dog trying to rid himself of a bad taste. Mappes growled his daily "Now turn to, you bastards," without emphasizing the *now* and the *bastards*. Then Bond was certain Mappes knew. That certainty quickened his blood.

From that time Mappes not only eased his weight; he got off the back of the division. Before, he'd spent virtually all his waking hours on the bridge; now he went below immediately after quarters, not caring whether the men turned to for the working day or not. Except when he had to put in an appearance above, he lay in his sack like a hurt animal. No more extra duty. No more disciplinary midwatches. No more prowling the bridge at night to see that the entire watch was present and alert.

At the same time Mappes quietly erased the symbols of authority. All of a sudden no coffee mug could be distinguished from any other. Mappes quit wearing a pair of rolled sema-phore flags through his beltloop. No mention of the missing long glass was ever made. Nor did Mappes reserve another for his own use.

Just as Mappes the division petty officer abdicated, Mappes the man changed. He reminded Bond of a superstitious savage trying to propitiate a vengeance he couldn't find or even com-prehend. Bond watched his frightened eyes, now darting, now avoiding, now fixing, as they tried to pin down the slippery form of suspicion. As though he were a sand statue a sidewalk artist was deliberately reshaping, Mappes' imperial form and arrogant face were remolded into the very type of cowardice and fear. Bond found himself taking a chilling delight in the writhings of Mappes. Toward Fels, whose brutishness and filth now scarcely offended, a reluctant loyalty almost became esteem.

*   *   *

The ship had been gone from her home port for more than a year. Almost two months had passed since the morning she'd steamed out of her most recent coral reef anchorage, the last spot of land her crew had seen. The kamikazes had stopped just before the typhoon—a month ago now. Still the great calm pre-vailed.

Day after day the sky was a cloudless stretch of blue, the sea a prairie of deeper blue. The darkness rolled in at night, out at morning without rocking the ship a degree or pitching it a second. From sunrise to sunset the carriers launched and landed their strikes of fighters, dive bombers, torpedo planes. But the enemy they hit never struck back. Sometimes Bond found himself doubting an enemy any longer existed.

At first the calm had seemed a blessing. They wished for nothing more than to go on that way. Life was reduced to a black sea at night, a blue sea in daylight. The same unending cycle. Then the old restlessness started again. This time nothing was the cause.

The fifth week of the calm brought strangeness. It began as a thirst. Leaning over the scuttlebutt one afternoon, Bond suddenly realized he'd been gulping water for maybe a minute. Then it occurred to him he'd been to the scuttlebutt five or six times within the hour. He resolved to pay attention to himself.

The rest of the afternoon, all that night, and all the next day, his thirst was unquenchable. He couldn't get down his food without floating it in great swallows of water. During the night he woke many times, his throat parched and burning, to crawl out of his sack and rush to the scuttlebutt for water.

As suddenly as it had come, the thirst disappeared. Other curious symptoms set in. For instance, although fleet speed was eighteen knots, Bond couldn't rid himself of the feeling that the ship was standing still. And his eyes began to see in single colors. For a certain period of time, usually five to ten minutes but once for as long as half an hour, everything turned the same color—the sky, the sea, the other ships in the task force, the decks and bulkheads on his own ship, the equipment on the signal bridge, even the bodies and faces of the officers and men aboard. The color varied. One time a blinding gold. Again, the blue of the sky or the sea. Another time the greenish silver of light between the moon and the ocean. And once, at midday, Bond's whole world turned black. Still another symptom—sudden unaccountable changes of body temperature. Sometimes at the very instant the tropic sun was sucking all moisture from his swollen tongue, Bond felt an arctic chill sweep through his blood. Again, while shivering in the tropic wind that rolled across the water between the sinking of the moon and the rising of the sun, Bond's body seemed fired with fever.

But worst was the little ball of steel. Like a metal heart broken loose from its vascular moorings, it whirled an orbit at some tremendous speed inside his chest. Eventually, accumulated centrifugal force would send it flying out through his flesh, like a piston through the block of an oil-dry engine.

As he stared at the glaze of ocean under the glaze of sky, Bond found himself thinking of those who had sailed the Pacific for centuries before coal and steam and diesel turbines. He imagined how they'd watched their sails hang languid days and weeks on end. He thirsted their thirst. Saw their phantoms. Knew their desperation. With them his madly becalmed spirit prayed for wind and cloud and rain. For currents and swells and hollows. For foam and spray. Bond even prayed for some manifestation of the enemy.

It seemed mere accident, that first night Bond and Fels stood by the hatch together. Olivio, Fels' relief, and Jensen, Bond's relief, had arrived on the bridge at precisely the same time. So Fels followed Bond. Under the lopsided moon. Down two ladders to the captain's deck. Down another ladder to the quarterdeck. Across the quarterdeck. Up the forecastle.

While the two of them stood waiting by the hatch above the sleeping compartment for the man climbing from below to reach the deck, Bond wasn't remembering that Mappes, a heavy sleeper and hard to awaken, was invariably the last man to relieve the watch. Fels moved to the starboard side of the hatch. Bond to port. Both slightly behind the hatch cover.

Bond was startled to see the face of Mappes rise from the blackness of the compartment into the darkness of the open night. His blood leaped forward with an obscure excitement. Neither Fels nor Bond stirred as they watched Mappes, drugged with sleep, amble down the forecastle and across the quarterdeck. When he passed beyond the forward bulge of the superstructure, Bond glanced across the hatch at Fels. Fels was staring after Mappes. A childlike grin on his brutish face. Climbing down the ladder, Bond felt Fels' grin behind him. In the blackness of the compartment it wore its old insinuation.

Leaving the bridge the next two nights Bond heard Fels footslog behind him. Both nights they took the same positions behind the forecastle hatch and waited for Mappes to ascend the ladder. Both nights just before Mappes stepped out on the deck Bond felt the "dog," a lead wrench used to secure the watertight cover on the hatch, being offered to his hand. Both nights he refused it.

The fourth night. Liquid sea seemed to have turned to ice and frozen the ship helpless. Close, full, directly overhead, the moon. It lighted out all the stars across the center of the sky. A green opaqueness, not color or tint but substance, above the sea.

Hearing Mappes' sluggish foot shake the ladder, Bond marked how furiously the little steel ball was whirling inside his chest. Suddenly he went dizzy, tottered. Gripping the dog Fels pressed into his hand for the third time, he steadied. The dog felt cold.

Mappes loomed like a miner coming up the collar of a shaft. Green from the light of the moon on the sea. As if he'd been hacking out emeralds. When Mappes' foot touched deck, Bond tapped him from behind with the dog. On the base of the skull. Very gently. Mappes swelled for an instant, as though waking from dead sleep, and Bond cursed himself for the lightness of the blow. But Mappes' bones folded up inside him. Soundlessly, gracefully, he settled on the deck.

Fels grinned as they hung over Mappes. Simultaneously they began to kick the body. And the head. While they kicked, both laughed. Then they stopped, as on signal. Fels kneeled and lifted Mappes. As though Mappes' flesh were weightless. Bond watched the thick-armed, dwarf-like Fels carry Mappes across the forecastle. At the lifeline Fels raised the body high over his head. Like a lifter pressing an easy weight. Then heaved him into the green darkness toward the darker water. Bond rushed toward the lifeline. He saw the silver-green hole in the ocean. It seemed to take a long while for the water to heal.

Bond sensed Fel's stare. Not at his face. At his right hand. Then Bond felt the dog burning his fingers. He tried to drop it over the lifeline. But couldn't. A current kept his fingers curled around the metal. All at once Fels slapped the dog from Bond's hand. It hissed as it fell toward the water.

Bond forced himself to look at Fels. The thick lips open. Not in a smile. As though trying to say a word. Vomit rifled up in Bond's throat. Swallowing, he plunged down the ladder into the sleeping compartment.

He lay in his sack. The sour taste almost suffocated him. An urge to climb to the forecastle and watch the sea from the lifeline. Not daring to, he checked the impulse. It came and went. A switch connected to his nerves being thrown on and off. Now a sweet hot exultation through his blood. Now a cold disgust.

No sense of time until he felt the first roll. So slight he couldn't be certain. Then another, and another. Soon he was sure.

For the first time since before the typhoon the general alarm sounded. Bond was the first man in the compartment on his feet. Climbing the ladder, he felt the ship pitching, too.

Just as he emerged on deck he heard the drone becoming a roar. Then glimpsed the streaking shadow, winged, close. As though shot from the sinking moon it slanted down on the port beam. All at once the superstructure exploded.

While they fought the fire, the storm harassed them. By midafternoon they'd won control. It was out just before dusk. By then the sea had calmed.

∗   ∗   ∗

All hands were assembled on the fantail. On one side the marine division stood in dress uniform, carbines at parade rest. Watches two and three of the signal division, also in dress uniform and at parade rest, on the other. In front, the ship's band, their instruments a blinding gold under the high tropic sun. Where three sections of the lifeline had been removed, the ship's carpenters had erected a low platform, and ranked along the platform, pitched outboard at a forty-five degree angle, were thirteen boxes, each draped with the national ensign. The boxes were also the work of the ship's carpenters. According to the corpsmen who had scraped up the seared flesh and allocated the blasted bones, there was no telling what belonged to whom.

The Protestant chaplain, a full commander displaying two long rows of campaign ribbons studded with bronze battle stars, stood staring at the sky. The Catholic chaplain, a surplice over his officer's khakis, worked his way down the row, signing the air over each coffin with the Cross. His lips were moving but none of the men could hear any words.

The band struck up the national anthem. Officers and men snapped to attention and uncovered. While the executive officer read out the names and ranks of the dead in a crisp voice, the crew held their hats over their hearts. After each name the executive officer read a citation awarding the deceased the Order of the Purple Heart. Division petty officer, signalman first-class Thomas Gundy Mappes, the ranking non-commissioned officer on the bridge at the time of the hit, was posthumously decorated with the Navy Cross—"for extraordinary heroism in operations against an armed enemy."

Hard on the final word of the executive officer's last citation the marine captain barked a command. The company of marines raised carbines. Another command. The carbines fired three salutes.

A big boatswain, who had been standing next to the Protestant chaplain, stumped across the platform. As the ship's bugler sounded retreat, the boatswain yanked out a shining belaying pin. The thirteen boxes slipped down the ramp toward the sea.

The sound of the bugle died across the water. A silent moment. The marine captain bawled an order. Trailing carbines, the company of marines marched off. Division officers commanded their men to replace hats, then dismissed them.

The second and third watches of the signal division dissolved from around Bond. All but Fels. He followed Bond across the fantail to where the ship's carpenters had already begun disassembling the platform. A couple of seamen from a deck division were replacing the lifeline. Bond stared at the sea, clear-blue, perfectly calm. He knew Fels was grinning beside him.

All at once Bond wheeled and headed for the forecastle. On each invisible footprint he dropped behind him he heard a thud. He felt one too. As if a steel ball were dropping down the bony ladder of his spine.

Answering Fire

SHE WAS NO MORE THAN FIVE FEET TALL. A WALKING
stump. Her steps were tiny and brisk. When she'd wiggled into
the upholstered chair in the inglenook at the far end of the bar,
the feet on her club legs scarcely touched the floor, though she
leaned forward rather than back, making her look tentative, out
of place. Beneath a dull brown skirt that fell halfway between
her knees and ankles, there seemed to be a single thigh. Everyone else in the room was part of either a couple or foursome.
She was the only one without a drink.

The bartender, a craggy-faced Yorkshireman who was dour as
a highland Scot, paid her no attention. Once situated, she laid
her hands on her lap, one on top of the other, as if covering or
concealing something. Daniel was sitting close enough to see
her eyes darting around to take in all they could without her
head turning. As they were about to glance at Alma and him, he
quickly looked away.

"Having another?" he asked.

"Sure, if you are," Alma replied.

Standing at the bar, half-facing the woman while he waited
for the bartender to refill their glasses, he saw that her hands

now were squeezed between the arm of the chair and the outside of her thighs. As he carried the fresh martinis back to
where Alma was sitting, he hoped the woman would notice and
come to understand the custom of the inn. He walked slowly, as
if careful not to spill a drop, and passed closer to her than was
necessary. When directly in front of her, he pulled back his lips
and crinkled his eyes ever so slightly. She could decide he either
was or wasn't directing a smile at her. Her face remained as
expressionless as a death mask.

The headwaiter from the dining room came striding in. Tall,
broad-shouldered, straight-backed, wearing a black serge suit
with gold buttons, he must have appeared intimidating to an
ill-at-ease foreigner. He distributed menus, in large maroon
leather covers, all around. When the woman unfolded hers, her
face disappeared behind it. Her hands were chunky with stub-
by fingers. She was short-armed.

"Dan, have you noticed the woman sitting alone beside the
fireplace?" Alma asked before opening her menu. "She must be
Chinese or Japanese or Korean. Or maybe she's from southeast
Asia somewhere."

"No," he lied. Why, he didn't quite know.

"Well, I've been watching her. She hasn't had a drink."

"Maybe she doesn't want one."

"Why else would she come into the bar?"

"God knows. Maybe she just blundered in."

"And sat down? When she could see everyone else drinking?
My guess is she can't figure out the procedure. Remember how
puzzled we were our first time here? We felt like intruders. I'll
bet she doesn't know what to make of the menu."

"Could be she has fluent English."

"I'm going to see whether she needs help."

"How's your Japanese?"

"No better than my Korean, Mandarin, Cantonese, or Thai."

As he watched Alma, still slender and straight-backed at seventy-five, approach the short, squat woman, he sipped his martini. While trying not to, he couldn't help overhearing the verbal thrust and parry as the couple beside him went at it.

"With or without the U.N., the cowboy's going in."

"But Saddam is a threat."

"Not to us or the Americans."

"He has weapons of mass destruction."

"They're not aimed at us."

"He could ignite the whole Middle East."

"Georgie lad has no more sense of history than the pony he's riding."

"Saddam Hussein's a madman. Suppose his uranium or chemicals land in the hands of terrorists?"

"We learned from Afghanistan. Twice. As well as in Iraq after World War I."

"Ancient history."

"What happened to the Russkies in Afghanistan is recent history."

"His father and Maggie ought to have gone all the way in '91."

"Bush will have a tiger by the tail. You'll see."

"Until Saddam's gone there's no hope of cleaning up the Israeli–Palestinian mess."

"Blair ought to know better than to hitch his wagon to a blazing comet."

"Well, whenever I have a chance I'll wave the dear old Union Jack and now's the time."

This last from a woman in late middle age with a tallowy face and a jaw that swiveled rather than dropped when she spoke. The words of the man, presumably her husband, sounded as if they were ground out by his teeth. To taunt him she broke into a chorus of "Rule, Britannia." Last evening he'd heard them spatting just as vigorously over whether tea was more properly poured into the cup before the milk, his position, or after, hers.

Back in the States the drums of war were being beaten so loudly and insistently and dismayingly that Alma and Daniel had cut and run—to be away for a couple of weeks, settled into a lovely village, which they'd visited many times, in North Yorkshire. Yet here "it" was, in the bar of their favorite inn, infiltrating his ear. At least, Daniel told himself consolingly, it wasn't being blared out on the evening news. No TV in the bars here.

"Well, I was right," Alma purred with a bit of self-satisfaction as she rejoined him. As if he'd seriously questioned her surmise. "The poor woman is baffled. So I explained how things work in the bar and that we order dinner here. She does understand and speak English well enough to get through to the waiter. Should we ask her to join us in the lounge afterward? I forgot to explain that's the convention for after-dinner coffee. I'm pretty sure she's Japanese."

While they ate he could hear the beating of the war drums across thirty-five hundred miles of ocean.

The woman left the dining room while they were waiting for their dessert. On her table he could see an empty wine glass.

*   *   *

"Have you heard the news on the telly this morning?" The little crown of white lace perched on top of the gray-haired head of their waitress brought back the nineteenth century. A white apron over a black dress constituted the rest of her uniform. Always pleasant and chatty, she was, they'd found out on one of their earlier stops at the inn, the wife of the sternly laconic bartender. The balance of opposites had held for many a year.

"Why, no," Alma replied. "Should we?"

"We've come to get away from the news," Daniel growled, taking care to sound like a good-natured dog awakened from a nap rather than a threatening bear.

"Oh, but this is such news as you'll want to know. They've bombed Baghdad, you Americans have, and Saddam Hussein and his sons have been killed. It was fearsome, they say. Our Royal troops have gone in too. God willing, it soon will be over."

As they made their way out of the dining room, they passed the woman at a table just inside the French doors. Facing the rest of the breakfasters, she ate with her head down.

* * *

"Have you heard the Japs have just bombed Oahu?" My mother, sister and I are having lunch in a restaurant close to a downtown hospital, where on the eleventh floor my father is pacing his room like a caged tiger. He's driven by the anxiety of what his doctor has called a nervous breakdown. Why all of a sudden at forty-nine he's been plunged into irrational fear and hopeless despair neither he nor we can understand.

I've never heard of Oahu.

"Our ships and the barracks at Pearl Harbor have been hit," the waitress goes on, "and lots of sailors and soldiers have been killed."

With doll-like prettiness and blond hair she wears pageboy,

like a movie star named June Allyson, she's not much older than
I am. If my mother weren't here, I'd try to find the courage to ask
her for a date.

When we've gone out onto Broad Street after hurriedly finishing lunch, I buy a newspaper from a boy yelling "Extry extry!
Japs attack Pearl Harbor! Roosevelt declares war!"

"Oh, what this will do to your poor father!" my mother half
sobs. "The poor man has more troubles of his own than he can
bear."

The next time I visit him, I see that my father has no emotion
to squander on the war.

*   *   *

"Early this morning, Near Eastern Time, American forces struck
Baghdad with three dozen Tomahawk missiles carrying one-
thousand-pound warheads. They were fired from naval units in
the Persian Gulf and the Red Sea. A Pentagon official has
announced intelligence has learned that senior Iraqi leadership was inside three targeted buildings at the time of the
attack. According to another U.S. spokesman, one unidentified
target was more important than the other two. He went on to
report that, after the missiles struck, a pair of F-17 fighters
dropped four two-thousand-pound bunker-destroying bombs
on an underground facility beneath one of the leveled buildings in which Saddam Hussein and two of his sons, Uday and
Qusay, were said by a reliable source to be hiding. According to
a later Defense Department report, the targets were obliterated
and some, if not all, the Iraqi leadership was killed. A C.I.A.
intelligence report cited witnesses who saw the body of Saddam Hussein being borne from the rubble on a stretcher.

"Subsequent attacks by Tomahawk missiles fired from war-
ships and by bombs dropped by hundreds of U.S. planes have
delivered a staggering blow to the Iraqi regime. According to
White House officials, the coordinated operation is intended to
shock and awe the government and war machine of Saddam
Hussein into a state of collapse. 'Shock and Awe' is the phrase
we keep hearing this morning out of Washington.

"Meanwhile here in London the War Department has reported that Royal Army troops, including the famed Desert Rats,
along with four thousand Royal Marines and units of the First
Armoured Division, have joined the U.S. Marines' First Expedi-
tionary Force. Landing from the Persian Gulf, they are rapidly
closing in on the strategically important city of Basra in southeast Iraq. Major General Robin Brims, in command of all Her
Majesty's forces in the region, including the First Armoured
Division, has announced . . ."

"Do you mind?" Daniel asked as he clicked off the television
set in their room. Considering that Alma had tuned into BBC
news despite the mutually agreed upon reason for their being
in this inn in Yorkshire at this time, he felt his mild irony was
justified.

"I was hoping the Brits might hold out, along with France and
Germany, and insist on having U.N. inspectors go back . . ."

"Never a chance. Look, we knew the dogs of war would be
unleashed. Let's not let it get to us. No more TV news, what
say?"

"Of course you're right. No sense having our noses rubbed in
what we've already sniffed. No more television for the duration
of . . . our temporary escape."

"Agreed. Unless BBC takes time out from showing the

destruction of Iraq to offering some footage of the test match in Melbourne."

* * *

When they entered the bar that evening, the woman was sitting in the same chair with a drink in her hand. Noticing Alma smile at her, he nodded, noncommittally. The woman, lifting herself by pushing on the chair arms, responded by half rising and bowing, holding her drink up like the torch of the Statue of Liberty.

"Don't you find it rather strange," Daniel began after they'd settled in with their martinis, "an Eastern woman halfway around the world from home, alone?"

While watching the dance of the gas-fed flame in the fireplace beside the woman's chair, the choreography of whose programmed flares he'd studied and diagrammed in his head, he was forcing himself not to hear what he knew was the conversation of his near neighbors.

"On the face of it, yes," Alma agreed. "Though when you consider how the world has changed since the end of World War II, maybe not so strange. Not only women in the West have been liberated, you know."

"True enough. But what can she be doing in a village on the edge of the North Yorkshire moors, where we're hiding out, you might say? It's not exactly London or Stratford-upon-Avon. Or Paris or Rome. Remember the hordes of Japanese we ran into in Stratford? Clicking their cameras and flashing light bulbs and posing. What on earth can they do with all those photographs and slides? Send them to friends and relatives who toss them away, as we do? Have slide show evenings, which we find excuses not to go to?"

" 'Hordes'? Of Japanese? Genghis Khan was a Mongol."

"Touché."

"They have a right to revere Shakespeare in their own way."

"Still, I think I'm on the right track. With Stratford-upon-Avon."

"Not sure what you mean."

"Our little friend's a teacher. No matter where she's from, you see a woman traveling alone, wearing sad-looking clothes, skirt halfway down her calf, hair in a double knot, you can be pretty damn certain you're looking at a schoolteacher."

"Oh my! More stereotyping. Every bit as bad as 'hordes.' Your notion of schoolmarms must be a carry-over from your childhood, which was, let me see, rather a few decades ago."

"Okay. I'm benighted. Hopelessly. No point in trying to enlighten me. Still, I'm convinced the lady is a teacher. Forget about her being an old maid because she's traveling alone. And about her self-presentation. Something emanates from her that says 'Japanese schoolteacher.'"

"From bad to worse. You've gone from stereotyping and fixation to clairvoyance."

"What'll you bet?"

"Though I have no strong feelings about her national origin, I'll take the bet. She's not a Japanese schoolteacher. For you, with your self-assurance, to win, she must be both. Winner chooses the restaurant in London the evening before we fly home. Price, no consideration. The tab goes on your credit card."

"No. On yours."

"You are sure. But actually I meant the generic 'your.' Whatever, how to find out? We can't just go up to her and ask. And she seems rather ill-at-ease to be forthcoming about herself."

"Leave it to me."

He was puzzled by his own certainty. And couldn't account for the attention he was giving the woman.

She'd finished her drink and, having ordered from the menu, had gone into the dining room before he and Alma had started on their second martini.

* * *

As they were passing through the hallway outside the bar, Daniel said, "Why not ask the lonely lady to have coffee with us, after dinner in the lounge, as you suggested last evening. You can explain the way it's done here, which you forgot to then. Remember? Maybe she's already figured it out. She seems to have caught on to procedures quite quickly. For an old maid schoolteacher from Japan."

"So, you're really determined to prove you're right. More to yourself than to me, it seems. Or maybe there's a glitzy restaurant in London you've had a secret hankering to dine in. Though you just might find yourself taking me to the Indonesian place near the Marble Arch that you dislike and I love. But why should I do the inviting? Why not you?"

"It was your idea to make her feel cozy in the first place. And if it's a woman thing, she'll feel more comfortable. She might think I'm coming on to her."

"No doubt, no doubt. A middle-aged schoolteacher young enough to be your daughter."

"Okay then. I'll ask her." He was surprised by his ready capitulation.

After entering the dining room, he broke away from Alma and went up to the table just inside the doorway.

"Good evening, madam." To address her formally and bow

slightly seemed called for. Still he felt as if he were playacting. "May I invite you to join my wife and me for coffee in the lounge after dinner?"

The little start she gave as she looked up from the bowl of soup her spoon was going into let him know she hadn't seen him approaching. Spoon in midair, she hesitated, then relaxed into a smile. Her teeth were discolored.

"I am honored to accept the kind invitation," she replied, jerking her head into a nod. But she didn't scoot back her chair and half rise, as he'd expected. On his way to join Alma it occurred to him that he ought to have added "or tea" after "coffee."

*   *   *

She did ask for tea. While sitting around a coffee table in the lounge, waiting for her pot and their French press to arrive, they exchanged names. Hers was Yuko Miyataka. Even though he and Alma had engaged in mock battle, primarily over his insistence that she was a schoolteacher, the fact that she was Japanese was of greater significance to him than her profession.

As Alma chatted her up about the loveliness of the village and the attractiveness and comforts of the inn, he studied her face, as if scrutiny might reveal what lay behind it. Her skin, the color of sun-baked mud, was slightly pitted. Narrowed by the plumpness of her cheeks, lumpy, like roughly molded clay, her eye sockets seemed to toe in. Making it appear you were looking at her, or she at you, from a distance, her black pupils were small. The top of her nose was flattened, widening her nostrils. In her upper lip was a deep indentation. She wore no makeup. She didn't exactly fit his picture of a geisha.

After the waiter had served them, Alma made the first thrust.

"I cannot help wondering what has brought you to York-shire." He was pleased that she hadn't used the first person plural.

"Oh, well, the great writers of this place."

He had to check an impulse to shoot a quick smile of triumph at Alma.

"Then I believe you are a teacher." Alma put it bluntly to confirm that she'd lost the bet.

"Oh sure. I teach the literature of English novel."

"Why are you not teaching now?" Given that she was conversing with a non-native speaker of English, Alma obviously found it appropriate to avoid contractions. "Is March not a school month in your country?"

"In March we are having school in Japan. You see, I have been given the leave of absence."

"So, you are engaged in research?"

"Oh no. Not the research. I am only the teacher."

They seemed to have reached a dead end. While they sat sipping in what he felt was a strained silence, he told himself the fact that Yuko Miyataka understood a word like "engaged" indicated that, despite some uncertainties in idiom, she was capable of keeping a conversation in English going. Which suddenly she did.

"You have read the novels of the famous Brontë sisters?" The question was directed to Alma.

"Yes. I have read *Jane Eyre* and *Wuthering Heights*. Many years ago. When I was a student in college." Alma was making her English sound as if she'd learned it from a book.

"Today I ride the coach to Scarborough. About one hour. I

wish to respect the grave of the youngest, named Anne Brontë. But I am not able to find it. Scarborough is a big city with many burial places."

"That must be a disappointment. When you have traveled so far. I have never read anything Anne Brontë has written. Have you, Dan?"

There was no way to escape Alma's ploy to involve him in the conversation.

"*The Tenant of Wildfell Hall.* That too was years ago. Anne wrote at least one other novel, it does seem to me." He heard his own idiom as unnatural.

Yoko Miyataka clapped her hands, smiled and nodded. There was a sweetness to her smile that eclipsed her lack of beauty. "The gentleman is very learned. Only one other. It has the title of *Agnes Grey*. Anne Brontë not so famous as her sisters."

"Will you pay your respects to them also?" Alma asked, to show her interest.

"Of course I must do that. But before, I must respect the grave of one other great writer. Not many miles from this village."

"Who is that?"

"Laurence Sterne, a fellow of infinite jest."

"A fellow of infinite jest?" Dan echoed before he could stop his tongue. "But that's Shakespeare. Yorick, in 'Hamlet.'" Sensing he was being rude to correct a woman from another culture so bluntly, especially a teacher of English, he wished he could unsay the words the instant they were out.

Again Yuko Miyataka clapped her plump hands, nodded and smiled. "Very good. And there is Yorick also in Laurence Sterne's novel *Tristram Shandy*. Very difficult to read for Japanese people."

Realizing Yuko Miyataka had tried to help him save face, Daniel felt a little flush of humiliation. And hearing her manage the l's and r's in "Laurence Sterne," "fellow," "Shakespeare," and "Yorick," usually so treacherous for Far Easterners, he had to admire her mastery of spoken English.

"I have never heard of it," Alma confessed. "Have you, Dan?"

"Yes, but I haven't read it. You say Sterne is buried near here?"

"Oh sure. Tomorrow I will ride the taxi to Coxwold village. It is fifteen minutes. That is where Laurence Sterne wrote and where is his grave."

"But the Brontës lived in Haworth," Alma put in. "We have been there. It is quite a distance."

"Then in two days more I will ride the coach to York city. One half hour when I came to here. Then I will ride the train to Leeds city. There I will ride the taxi to Haworth village. I will respect the graves of Charlotte and Emily Brontë and I will see into the museum. It was the home where they did their writings. These are important for me to teach the Japanese students their greatness."

"I have very much admiration for you," Alma said reverently. "For your commitment and your courage."

Daniel wondered whether Yuko Miyataka had understood "commitment." But again she nodded and beamed her sweet smile.

Back in their room neither Daniel nor Alma mentioned their bet. Now that he'd been proved right on both counts, he'd persuade her, when they'd reach London, that his choice was the Indonesian restaurant he didn't care for. To counter the condescension she'd be certain to feel, he'd insist the tab go on her credit card.

* * *

A chronic insomniac, he awakened in the grip of depression. The red numbers on the face of the digital clock said 1:22. If he'd been dreaming, he couldn't recall what. He knew the martinis were a component of the chemistry that was keeping him from sleep. As he confronted the prospect of hours of restlessness, he heard Alma breathing with a regularity indicative of a state of blessed unconsciousness. He was lying on his right side. After rolling onto his left, dropping onto his back, flipping onto his belly, squirming onto his right side again, stretching full-length, then doubling his knees and hunching over them, he found himself saying to himself the names of the international code of flags at sea.

Able, Baker, Charlie, D...., Easy, Fox, George, How, Item, Jig, King, L...., Mike, Nan, O...., Peter, Queen, Roger, S...., Tare, Uncle, Victor, W...., X-ray, *Yoke, Zebra.* Five flag names he couldn't remember. When he ran back through, he came up with "Love," "Oboe," and "Sugar." Without succeeding, struggle as he might, in dredging up the words for "D" and "W," he drowsed off.

Reawakening at a few minutes past four, he flattened himself on his back. When he closed his eyes, the darkness of the room became a blank slate. Gradually it dawned on him that the two letters whose code names he hadn't been able to come up with were the initials of his name.

* * *

"Have . . . one . . . suburb . . . of . . . Pittsburgh . . . in . . . tow . . . full stop . . . awaiting . . . instructions . . . end of transmission."

Dean, signalman first class, is reading flashing light from the *Hornet,* two or three miles off our port bow. I take the words down on a clipboard. The message is addressed to the admiral aboard. It's dated Je 9, '45. We've just ridden out a four-day typhoon off the coast of Kyushu. This morning the sea is smooth enough to deserve its name—Pacific.

"What in Christ's name does that mean?" Dean growls. "I'm going to ask for a repeat. Whitlock, read the son of a bitch with me."

"'Have one suburb of *Pittsburgh* in tow.' That's what he's saying, Dean."

"Don't make no Goddamn sense," Dean grumbles as he carries the message off to the admiral's chief of staff in flag plot.

At chow Dean fills me in. "The fucking storm split the bow off the *Pittsburgh* and her watertight doors kept it afloat. The *Hornet* spotted it, pulled alongside, put a man aboard that secured a hawser on a bollard and they took the fucker in tow. Their captain's asking Old Ironsides what the fuck to do with it. Nobody don't know where the hell the rest of the fucking cruiser is."

* * *

Waiting to see a crack of light between the draperies across the bedroom window, he recalled how welcome the wit of the *Hornet*'s captain had been during a harrowing time and how remarkable the recovery and repair of the *Pittsburgh*. Both parts were towed back to Pearl Harbor, where, after being welded together, she became seaworthy again. Yet the severity of that typhoon was eclipsed, he remembered, by the destructiveness of the typhoon they'd gone through, literally, the previous

December in the South China Sea, off the coast of Luzon in the Philippines.

And the kamikazes. At first our command had construed the planes' plunging into ships as unintentional, the result of the pilot's inability to control his aircraft after it had been hit by anti-aircraft fire. Gradually it dawned on those at the top that these were planned suicide missions, not even instantaneous decisions, like that of Captain Colin Kelly, the first U.S. hero in the Pacific theater, where in the early months of the war we were suffering one defeat after another. Rather than bail out, he'd guided his stricken fighter plane into the superstructure of a Japanese battleship. What irony—the first kamikaze was an American.

The admiral aboard his ship, Annapolis '07, appropriately nicknamed Old Ironsides, came up with a counter to the devastating new Japanese tactic. In addition to our twelve-inch signaling lamps, we carried four thirty-six inch carbon-arc searchlights. Their function was to locate enemy aircraft at night and illuminate them as targets for our twenty and forty-millimeter antiaircraft batteries. After Pearl Harbor we'd quickly learned that, logical as the theory was, its use was both futile and self-defeating. Guided by hand, the lights couldn't locate and track fast-moving aircraft in the dark, while they made the ships that were showing them visible targets for high flying bombers and skimming torpedo planes. From that time on, no light aboard ship was permitted to be visible between sunset and sunrise.

Old Ironsides, with enough gold braid on his uniform to change a designated procedure, concluded we could defeat the kamikazes by picking them up visually, after radar had located and fixed on them, with our thirty-six inch lamps' powerful beams, which would confuse and blind the pilots as they made their dive or run. The Japanese rode the streams of light we provided smack into their targets. After two ships were hit in rapid succession, that tactic was abandoned. Old Ironsides remained in command of our task group.

*   *   *

Water-borne armadillos, we're prowling the South China Sea for prey—whatever remnants of the battered Japanese fleet might be foolhardy enough to show themselves. Or a freighter, slow and low in the water, her lading meant for lands that the Japs have taken, a sitting duck for the guns of a man-of-war— you might say an albatross if freighters had wings and ships still carried crossbows.

A brilliant sun. On the signal bridge I'm scouring the space just above the horizon, a seam between the paler blue of sky and the darker blue of ocean. In the lens of a long glass my eye picks up a black speck. Its blip on the radar screen, I hear through the earphones of the headset I'm wearing, is too small to identify.

I push the button that brings to life the speaker my lips are almost touching. "Small craft at four o'clock. Distance approximately two miles. Looks dead in the water. Probably fishing boat."

Target confirmed by my eye, I'm blinded for an instant by a flash as the five-inch mount only feet from my right eardrum blasts off. In the glass I see a straddling of water spouts a pod of whales might jet around the speck which has disappeared.

They never knew what hit them. No need to expend main-battery sixteen-inch shells on such small game. In these waters it couldn't possibly have been Japanese, was most likely Vietnamese or Filipino. Still, even the humblest native craft might radio our presence and position. We can't afford to take chances. Or prisoners. Think of it as baptism, of water and fire at once.

*   *   *

It came back to him in the dark—the first war crime in which he'd been a participant. Next time there had been less anguish. And the next and the next, diminishing. He closed his eyes and shuddered. In the still darker dark a circle of blue shone brightly enough to make his inner eye want to look away. If only his bodily eyes would open. The lids refused to go up. Within the blue, either sea or sky, he saw the ribbed hull of a scallop-shaped fishing boat. Inside was a cargo of white bones. Above it hovered a host of human shapes—children, wives, parents, he knew they were, heads bowed in submission or prayer, arms flung up in horror or supplication, mouths rounded as if moaning or exclaiming, eyes lowered in grief or despair.

Summoning all his will, he lifted his eyelids and stared into the less dense dark of the room. "Unfortunately we had to," they'd told themselves while doing. "Had to" now was his story, a memory for himself, a record for posterity that provides justifications. What the boy-sailor, a moral virgin until then, had done, his necessity, carrying out the commands of Old Ironsides, he'd buried in his mind as many fathoms deep as the little boat lay in the gulf of oblivion. Sooner or later it had to have happened—some outside force was bound to shatter the concealment of time and distance, the waters of the grave would part, and the boat with its cargo of bones would rise into his consciousness.

Guilt can't be bought off, satisfied by remorse. He knew he

harbored no retroactive willingness to swap his billet aboard a man-of-war, fifty-five thousand displacement tons of armor and weapons, for a nameless fisherman's berth on a timbered unarmed boat. What penance then is an unmanned man to do when it's generations too late for reparation?

Ought he pay the *New York Times* to make public his mea culpa and a plea for forgiveness in a full-page spread, with one photograph of him then in uniform, another of him now in sackcloth and ashes? Would a home-page on the Internet provide greater exposure?

Ought he fly to Vietnam, with an exaction of its own, make a barefoot pilgrimage, stumping the final mile on his knees, to the village of My Lai, first land west of the fishing boat's watery grave, prostrate himself in whatever the burial ground there, and fast until he'd be nothing but skeleton?

Ought he make his way to the leper colony on Culion, Isle of the Living Dead, a dab of arid earth off Palawan in the Philippines, due east of the unmarked sea in which the fishing boat had vanished, and like San Juan de Cruz press lips against the lesions of "the living dead"?

Why shift it off to somewhen somewhere else? What better time and place than here and now, where and when the cover of distance and time have been breached? Come morning he could present himself to the rector of the parish church, hand him a document that would commit him to give all he had to the parish poor, the widowed, the orphaned, and to spend the remainder of his days celibate, praying and fasting.

If only he could love the souls of six—or were there nine or a dozen or more who had been aboard that boat—men he never knew. Oh, the futility of babbling lamentations!

*   *   *

Scout planes have radioed that we're steaming directly toward a powerful typhoon. A quartermaster lets it leak that by altering course twenty degrees to the north we can skirt what for us will not be a divine wind.

"Damn the typhoon," I hear Old Ironsides, striking an original heroic phrase, bark at his chief of staff in the passageway between flag plot and the shelter on the signal bridge. "We'll steam between her thighs and break into her cunt at the center, then batter our way out of her arms. Engines to thirty knots."

As surprised as I am that a man I consider scarcely literary can strike a metaphor, I'm shocked to hear an admiral use the word "cunt."

"All hands on deck," blares over the PA system.

The wind has begun to roar. Water becomes a gargle of sea and rain. Spray, thick and heavy as waves, stings what's exposed of my face, cowled by oilskin gear. On deck we've slung lines between railings and stanchions. Clinging to them, as I make my way hand over hand against gusts, burns the skin on my palms. When I measure the wind's force by leaning full weight against it, it holds me up. At first it's exciting.

From time to time I poke my head into the signal shelter. Eyes bugging, I watch the swinging of the pendulum of the clinometer—27° starboard, 26° port, 28° starboard we're rolling. At thirty, hull over stacks we go, Dean, who's mocked me by saying he's worn out more sea bags than I have socks, has told me. Maybe he's yarning, maybe not. When I check the log, I find the anemometer reads 157 m.p.h.

Hearing over TBS that the storm's breath has blown a seaman

off the flight deck of the *Intrepid,* I make out through the swirl of sea and rain a destroyer, the *Monaghan,* more shark-like than savior-like, prowling the circle that describes his liquid grave. Now sea heaves itself as high as the captain's bridge. Everyone hugs inboard bulkheads. Although even old salts, including Dean, are seasick, it hasn't come nigh me.

Word seeps out from flag plot we're battling the worst blow Old Ironsides has run afoul of since he was a midshipman. When he shows himself on deck, gold-braided cap off so his thinning gray hair is swept back by the wind, as I imagine Ahab's or an Old Testament prophet's would be, it's evident he's relishing the encounter. For the old bastard or the task unit he commands, except the ship I'm on, I wouldn't give a rusty piss. Fear has shriveled my prick to an earthworm. Nobody jokes. I realize I'm a born coward.

During what should be daylight, visibility is less than at dusk. When neither she nor us is dropped in a trough, I can barely make out the ghostly silhouette of the *Monaghan.* Since Old Ironsides has ordered the formation to tighten up, I judge she can't be more than the length of a football field at two o'clock off our starboard bow, rolling and pitching like a whale in its death throes. We plummet into a deep gorge. Then when we're flung on top of a mountain that would take eons to form on land, I look and wait for the *Monaghan* to reappear. She never does. Swamped, she's turned into a submarine who's made her final plunge.

Over TBS comes a report her sister destroyers, the *Hull* and the *Spence,* have also been swallowed, hundreds of unwitting kamikazes aboard. Unfathomable. Piloted by the unmalleable will of Old Ironsides, we blunder through to deal more death.

I imagine the three armor-plated coffins. Inside each is a contortion of bodies, which moments ago were snapping and obeying commands and performing assigned duties. Their resting place is the bottom of the South China Sea. In the ear of my mind I hear the descending voice of Lawrence Tibbett, which I'd listened to as a child when the needle clutched by the hand of the tone arm went spinning through the grooves of a seventy-eight r.p.m. bakelite record on the rosewood victrola in the parlor of my family home:

"Rocked in the cradle

of

the

deep."

At this moment I'd give an arm, literally, yes, a leg, to be back there. Because of the wind's roar I don't have to stifle the childish sob I feel rifling up my throat.

* * *

He was having a bad night of it, very bad. The bed was a ping-pong table and he was being batted from awakenedness to sleep to awakenedness, from present to past to present, from where he was to where he'd been to where he was. Having fallen into a doze at a few minutes past four, after having gone through the South China Sea typhoon, he awoke at a few minutes past six to find himself tapping numbers in Morse code on his thigh: dot dot dot dot dash—four; dot dot dot dot dot—five; dash dot dot dot dot—six . . .

When he reached ten he made himself stop tapping, but went on counting, slowly. Carrier planes. One of his duties had been to record the number of aircraft in a strike as, bomb-laden, they were catapulted off the flight deck of one of the carriers their task unit was protecting. Hours later he'd record the number that returned. Then subtract.

Off Luzon, during the retaking of the Philippines, the kamikazes had struck erratically. During the invasion of Iwo Jima, where the invading troops desperately needed naval and air support, the suicide attacks accelerated to a steady flow. In mid-March, off Kyushu, Japan's southernmost island, the *Franklin,* the closest carrier in the task unit formation, her flight deck filled with loaded planes about to take off, was hit. Her bombs, ammunition and fuel exploded into flames that lit up the sky like a Fourth of July fireworks display. To watch with irresistible fascination human torches leaping from the hell of the flight deck into the sea brought tears salted with fear that scalded his cheeks. For eight hours the *Franklin* committed slow suicide. Next morning she was a smoldering hulk.

Some of the roasted bodies still alive enough to writhe and scream with pain, plucked from the sea by destroyers, were ferried to his ship, hoisted by boom, block and tackle onto the forecastle, then carried below to sick bay for whatever immediate treatment and relief the medical staff could administer. The metal stretchers on which they'd been transported were returned to the forecastle. There powerful hoses were played on their steel mesh to flush off shreds of scorched skin and charred flesh, morsels of beef cleaned from the grille of a hibachi.

During the month-long battle for Okinawa in April '45, kamikazes sank twenty destroyers on the picket line. More than a hundred and fifty other ships were severely damaged.

On the signal bridge a grim joke was going the rounds. He'd heard the format in junior high school, only later had realized the initiating questions and answers echoed the monologue of the sleepy porter when he answered the knocking on the gate of Macbeth's castle the night King Duncan was murdered.

"Knock, knock."

"Who's there?"

"Chicken."

"Chicken who?"

"Chicken Teriyaki."

"Who the hell is Chicken Teriyaki?"

"The only kamikaze pilot who'll survive this fucking war."

The laughter was hollow. When Blessington relayed the joke to Gallup, Gallup responded by grabbing Blessington by the shirt front, slamming him against a bulkhead, and twisting the chambray cloth so tight that Blessington squealed for help. It took Pettinghill, Mirski, and Catherman to pry Blessington, gasping and red-faced, loose. "It's a joke, for Chrissake," he whimpered as he went slinking off.

One afternoon our antiaircraft batteries, stressed, frightened, edgy, took down two U.S. fighters engaged in a dogfight with some Zekes, probably kamikazes. Neither pilot survived the friendly fire. Two replicas of the Stars and Stripes were not painted on the outside bulkhead of the captain's bridge to join the line of Rising Suns that served to keep score of the enemy we'd killed.

It trickled down the chain of command that, after the first beachhead had been established, it was touch and go on Okinawa. To provide stronger air support, the bomb loads carried by the carriers' TBF's were increased. On one memorable morning one out of every half dozen or so aircraft catapulted from the carrier he was keeping track of failed to get the necessary lift as it left the flight deck and went plunging nose-down into the drink. For hours destroyers circled, searching for those who'd managed to extricate themselves from their harness and wriggle out of the cockpit of their submerged planes. He estimated that less than half were rescued.

With chilled awe he remembered those airmen on the carriers. Knowing whose and how many seats at mess in the wardroom and bunks in their sleeping quarters were empty, they'd watch the plane ahead of them in line take off, nose down, and disappear. Then they'd taxi their own plane into position to be catapulted to potential death by drowning. How could they do it? Were they too not kamikazes, willing to give up their own lives for a chance to kill the enemy? If they were, along with the pilots shot down by their own guns and those burned to death from their own explosives aboard the stricken *Franklin* and those buried inside the *Monaghan, Spence* and *Hull,* was every airman, soldier, marine, and sailor, including him, also a breath of the death-dealing Divine Wind?

But at least our "kamikazes" had a chance, he reminded himself, not for the first time. Only eight or nine hundred men needlessly went down in the typhoon, ironic as "only" and shameful as "needlessly" were. Our guns destroyed many fewer of our own planes than Japanese. Most of our pilots lifted off the flight deck and flew into the blue to deliver their loads of killing fire without being taken down by Japanese antiaircraft batteries or gunners on Japanese planes, their opposite comrades-in-arms. Those who failed to get airborne at least had roughly a fifty–fifty chance of freeing themselves and being fished from the sea by a searching destroyer.

But the Japanese kamikaze took off knowing he was not to

return. He recalled a night when he was stretched out, frightened and weary, expecting general quarters to sound at any second, commanding him to leap out of his bunk, scoot up the ladder from his compartment, race across the forecastle, and climb to the signal bridge. Night after night, to work their nerves and deprive them of sleep when they were already worn down by repeatedly alternating five hours on and off watch, Japanese planes, flying above the range of their antiaircraft fire, would drop tinfoil that showed up on the radar screen as flocks of bogeys. That night, while waiting, he'd tried to imagine himself as a Japanese kamikaze, about to take off on what was certainly his last mission, perhaps his first. "Duty is heavier than a mountain," he still remembered reading somewhere, would be the imperial rescript written on his brain, "while death is light as a feather." He hadn't been able to put himself inside his enemy.

*   *   *

A gorgeous morning. On the surface of the water you can track the wake of flying fish for yards. Sea and sky are vying for the purity of all blues. Clarity of air means unlimited vision to the horizon. Sun is a wafer dipped in red wine. "Red in the morning, sailors take warning." Our carrier planes are off striking Japanese ground installations on Kyushu.

All at once the peace is broken by the popping of ack-acks. Glasses to eyes, I'm scanning the quadrant from zero to ninety degrees starboard. On the way back to zero, I pick up a plane, skimming the water to stay beneath the waves of our radar.

"Zeke approaching at two o'clock," I shout into the mouthpiece of my headset. "Closing fast."

Undeterred by the swarms of twenty and forty-millimeter

shells our antiaircraft batteries let fly, the plane keeps coming. It's close enough for me to see its nose, targeted on the signal bridge, on me.

"Still closing fast!" I yell.

All at once I've been shot headfirst from the mouth of a five-inch gun. Zooming toward the plane, along with a stream of red tracers, I can make out a goggled and helmeted head behind a plexiglass windshield. Suddenly over the racket of the twenties and forties, I hear the blast of five-inch guns. I know I'm on the bridge, paralyzed, but I can't feel the deck beneath my feet, I know I'm screaming "still close . . . " but I can't hear my voice.

Now there's nothing to see but endless blue and the red sun, nothing to hear but silence.

* * *

As he lay hopelessly awake, sleep-deprived not by dropped Japanese foil but by gin-fueling and history-feeding machinery in his brain he couldn't switch off, he found himself trying again, six decades later, to imagine what would have been his state of mind on the morning just before, had he been the one to take off on a death flight. Quietly, careful not to disturb Alma, whose brain had no such machinery and contained no such pernicious material, he slipped from bed. Fumbling at the night stand, he felt out his glasses and the tablet and pen the inn provided beside the telephone. Then he tiptoed into the bathroom, slowly closed the door to keep it from creaking, turned on the light, and slipped on his glasses. After relieving himself, he sat down on the toilet seat. Making use of his scant, romantically clichéd notion of things Japanese, he began writing. The words were waiting to spill out.

"After three days inform my father, gem merchant in Kyoto: 'In the month of the ripening plum he answered the summons of the Rising Sun without sorrow.' To my mother convey this empty urn, enameled with gulls on the wing. Speak no word. Bow three times and retire. Do not search for the girl with oval hands and lustrous eyes.

"Here in moonlight, ahead of dawn, stands the raven-winged plane that will burst into flame. May the birds on the back of the giant eagle it is my duty to destroy be pregnant with eggs that will consume their mothers and the father eagle with them.

"Sometimes when you light the ceremonial tapers and scatter incense before your sons, remember, my friend, how we locked fingers here, last human touch. Not yet twenty, I fly to greet the sun and dive."

"At last," he murmured to himself as he crawled back into bed. Within minutes he fell into sleep.

*   *   *

Reveille has sounded over the PA system. Minutes later, in the light of false dawn, I'm standing in ranks on the signal bridge, still groggy with sleep. Ensign Farnham is calling muster in a voice shrill as a bosun's whistle.

"Argersinger . . . Blessington . . . Dean . . . Gallup . . . Mirski . . . Pettingill . . . Vincenti . . . Webster . . . Whitlock . . ."

Hearing my name jars me fully awake. "Ho, sir," I sing out. The top of a fireball, which is either the sun or an aircraft carrier bursting into flames, is just becoming visible on the eastern horizon.

＊　＊　＊

He awoke to a sliver of light between the draperies. When he and Alma entered the dining room for breakfast, he immediately looked at her table. Empty. Most likely she was already off to "respect" Laurence Sterne's grave. Sometime he'd have to read *Tristram Shandy.*

Craving a shot of caffeine to counter sleep deprivation and, he hoped, rally him to contend with the despair that had him by the throat, he pushed down on the plunger of the French press the instant the waitress let go of the handle, poured Alma, then himself a full cup of coffee.

"Have a rough night?" Alma asked, as he took a long swig even though the liquid was burning his tongue. "You should give it a couple of minutes to mix. That'll make it stronger."

"No need to let it stand. That's the mystery of a French press. Brews in an instant. Thoroughly." He swilled more coffee.

"Doesn't seem possible. Think of the time it takes a percolator. Or a drip."

From the nearest tables he could hear what for the English, who had a tendency to mumble and who in the dining room at breakfast would pitch their conversation almost to a whisper, were perfectly audible voices. Certain he knew what was inciting them, he refused to allow his brain to process their words. To hold his own in a skirmish with Alma over the virtues of various methods of brewing coffee was beyond his power. Bruised, shaky, paralyzed, he gave in to silence.

"I suppose Yuko's had early breakfast and already's off to 'respect' the tomb, wherever it is, of that writer whose name I can't seem to remember who wrote a novel I've never heard of.

Don't you find me a perfect blend of ignorance and loss of short-term memory?"

The sound of the name "Yuko" gave him a shake. Well-intentioned as Alma was in trying to divert him from himself by making what she believed was small talk, she was asking him to address a subject which, so early in the morning after a dreadful night, he'd prefer not to. Yet he hadn't the heart not to respond.

"That writer's Laurence Sterne. The title of his novel is *Tristram Shandy*. It's a classic. The name of the village, I think, is Cock's Wold. You know how eccentric English place names seem to us."

"Oh the blessed fortune to be hitched to a star that displays learning like a shower of meteorites. How does that blazing metaphor strike you, Mr. Luminary?" Coming on as though he were a literary historian did make him an inviting target. "What say we drive to Cock's Wold and respect Laurence Sterne's grave? Could be that would seduce me into reading . . . *Tristran Sandy*. That's not quite right, is it? Whatever, we might run into Yuko and we could lunch with her in the local pub."

He had no intention of seeming to be following Yuko Miyataka and traipsing through the parish churchyard, searching for the grave of Laurence Sterne. The reason was . . . well, the reason had to be akin to why he'd lied when Alma had asked whether he'd noticed the woman sitting alone in the bar without a drink the previous evening.

"To be honest, I've been looking forward to watching the delayed tape of the test match between Australia and Sri Lanka on the telly. If it's on."

*   *   *

Alma was ensconced in the window seat, reading the *Guardian*. He'd vowed not to look at a newspaper for the duration of their A.W.O.L. Unable to get his mind off what he imagined was going on in Iraq, he was slumped in a Chippendale wing chair, only his eye attending to the match on the TV screen. Suddenly his full attention was grabbed by a powerful stroke from a Sri Lankan batsman. The camera was following the flight of the ball toward the boundary. Then it shifted onto the Aussie at long-leg racing toward it. Leaping like a grasshopper, he thrust out his right arm and snatched in his palm what surely would have been a six.

Still stretched out, he crashed onto the green, doubled up, rolled over three times, and lay still. The downed man's teammates raced into the frame and surrounded the player motionless on the grass. In their whites they looked like a team of doctors consulting over a patient. As the camera withdrew, in a long perspective they blurred to a single white shape, a fallen parachute ballooning above the surface of a body of water.

* * *

General quarters has sounded. I race from my compartment, where I've been folding wash on my sack, up the ladder, out the hatch, across the forecastle, up the ladders to the signal bridge. Sky is an endless prairie of blue, sea a field of deeper blue. Manning a long glass on a swivel, I slip on my headset and commence scanning a quadrant off the starboard beam, air space that's my responsibility. My eye picks up and focuses on a bomber at low altitude.

"Betty four o'clock starboard, elevation 30°, approximate distance a half mile," I shout into the mike hanging around my neck. "Betty closing fast at four o'clock . . ." My voice is drowned out even to my own ear by the chattering of two twenty-millimeter antiaircraft guns directly below me. All the forties on the starboard side are also crackling.

Suddenly a puff of black smoke trails from the tail of the Betty. Two parachutes, white handkerchiefs signaling "we surrender," open behind the plane. Letting the doomed aircraft pass out of the lens of my long glass, I focus on the body dangling from one of the parachutes. Guns are still spitting out shells. All of a sudden there is no body, just dangling shreds. The firing doesn't stop as the unmanned chute continues its slow descent. Nor does it end when the chute softly kisses the water and collapses to a small white mushroom bobbing like a patch of plankton. Shells are being pumped into a man who no longer is, is not even a corpse. They're riddling mere fabric. Then silence.

* * *

Even though he felt vomit about to rifle up his throat, still he couldn't help re-experiencing a giddy elation over the destruction of a plane and its crew whose mission had been to bomb his ship, intending to kill him.

Then he recollected that full recognition of the war crime he'd abetted by discharging his duty hadn't come until a year later. War over, honorably discharged, he was being rewarded for his services by a grateful government with the benefits of the G.I. Bill of Rights. He'd returned to the university in which he'd been a freshman when, prompted by conscience to fight against the Nazis, not the Japanese, he'd enlisted in the Navy and after a stint in communications school had found himself in the Western Pacific.

For a class in world literature he'd been reading the *Iliad*. At the desk in his room, light thrown by a gooseneck lamp, he'd come to Homer's account of the behavior and emotions of Achilles during the killing of Hector. Daniel's eye could still see Achilles stripping the armor from his enemy's lifeless body, repeatedly stabbing the corpse with the point of his spear, tying the carcass to the axle of his chariot, then dragging what had been Hector around the walls of Troy for the eyes of the dead man's mother and father to behold.

Etched in Daniel's brain were the words with which Homer had had Achilles reveal to the dying Hector his impulse to revert to cannibalism: "Would that my heart's desire could so bid me to carve and eat your raw flesh." Sitting before a television screen in a room in an inn in Yorkshire fifty-seven years later, he felt again the shudder of horror that had come over him in his dormitory room that night as the connection suddenly had sparked.

*　*　*

The Aussie at long-leg who had made the amazing catch was hobbling on one foot, arms around the shoulders of two teammates, toward the pavilion. Shaking his head to bring himself back to here and now, Daniel turned toward Alma, immersed in the *Guardian,* and stared at her for reassurance—reassurance for what, he couldn't say. Just reassurance. Then while waiting for play to be resumed, he leaned his head back on the top of the chair and shut his eyes. Within seconds he heard a loud cheer. Raising his eyelids, he saw the hand on the right arm of the injured player raise itself from the shoulder of one of his teammates and wave. This heroic gesture increased the cheer to a roar.

*   *   *

"Now hear this, now hear this. At eight zero one five this morning, a 4.5 ton device with the unprecedented force of 20,000 tons of TNT was dropped on the city of Hiroshima on the island of Honshu. Preliminary reports indicate that massive damage was inflicted on the target."

A roar of exultation explodes from every man of us on deck, from lieutenant commander to seaman. Someone claps me on the back, hard. Wheeling around, I look into the grinning blubbery face of Gallup, who hails from Frog Pond, Tennessee, and had once called me, not a damn Yankee, but a "Goddamn mother-fucking Yankee." Catherman, so fat he huffs and puffs and turns beet-red climbing a ladder, and Vincenti, the smallest and oldest inductee in the division, who shamelessly weeps every evening over his wife and daughter back in Perth Amboy, are jitterbugging together. Thompson and Zelinski, who, glutted with warm beer, had bloodied and battered the features of each other's face with their fists on the coral reef island named Mog Mog, Ulithi, during a three-hour liberty we'd been granted between Iwo Jima and Okinawa, are embracing like eleven-year-old girls. Cragg, who had never been out of Flat Rock, Alabama, before he'd been drafted, snatches off his white hat, flings it onto the deck, as if to say, I'm done with you forever, then, letting out a rebel whoop of jubilation, tramples it as he dances an impish jig.

Sounding like a grand pipe organ, the ship's horn blasts three short and one long peal of triumph. Body feeling light enough to fly, I let go a full-throated cry of joy and playfully poke Gallup, whom I loathe, in the ribs.

*   *   *

He recalled the controversy in 1995 over displaying the Enola Gay, named with what would be an oedipal pathos, were it not so bitterly ironic, for the mother of the pilot of the plane that had dropped the bomb, called Little Boy— litotes to beat all litotes— as part of the exhibition mounted by the Smithsonian Institution to commemorate the fiftieth anniversary of the destruction of Hiroshima. Above the mellow tones of the commentators when the cricket match was resumed in Melbourne, fifty-eight years after how many mothers and little boys had been incinerated and doomed and disfigured in the blink of an eye, he heard a jumble of voices in his head clamoring for his attention.

Still immersed in the *Guardian,* Alma seemed not to notice that he got up, crossed to his night stand, again picked up tablet and pen, and returned to his chair. He supposed she supposed he was still watching and listening to the match. Neither the images of the game nor the commentary on it distracted him. After many false starts, much crossing out and rewriting, he managed to sort out the voices he still was hearing.

> I turned to a clinker that burned ten years before consuming itself.

> Still simmering, I have scoriae for fingers, a blister where my left breast ought to be.

> We, the lucky ones, flashed and burned out, Roman candles, sparklers, Catherine wheels, celebrating your

Fourth of July a month and two days late.

I, pilot of the weather plane that scouted the skies over Hiroshima and gave the all clear to the Enola Gay for letting Little Boy fall—beyond forgiveness, denied rest, haunted, drifting, an outcast, cashiered, committed, all those charred and radiant bones lashed to my back, the lament of a ghostly choir of a hundred thousand souls humming in my ear.

In unison we cry: bury the bird that dropped the egg of fire. Exhibit us.

*   *   *

As the cricket players became no more than moving images on a screen, he knew his eye was losing interest in the match. Shame and remorse were carrying his mind back to his effort to contend with the accelerating guilt he'd felt while reading John Hersey's *Hiroshima* after returning from the war, anything but a conquering hero. He remembered telling himself that at that moment of spontaneous celebration he'd really had no way of comprehending the enormity of what had happened.

Besides, his own life, he'd been convinced then, had been at stake. He'd experienced the ferocity of the Japanese resistance, had witnessed the sinking of destroyers, the kamikaze attacks that had killed and burned and maimed his comrades-in-arms on carriers, cruisers and battleships. Reports of the cruelty of the Japanese military to those they'd conquered and of their barbarous treatment of prisoners of war he'd believed were more than propaganda churned out by the films he'd been exposed to, which heavy-handedly divided the globe into two worlds, the light and the dark, the good and the evil, the Allies and the Axis. Hadn't the Japanese allied themselves with Hitler and treacherously attacked Pearl Harbor?

In the "pony" editions of *Time*, which were passed from hand to hand, he'd read that the Japanese had held countless planes back from combat, had stockpiled ammunition along the entire coast of its home islands with an unbroken line of shore batteries, that a million ground troops, some battle-hardened, some fresh, as well as every able-bodied old man and boy, and thousands of women, had dedicated themselves to fight to the death against the invasion of their homeland, scheduled to commence in November. The forces he was a part of were still depleted and exhausted from the battles of the Philippines, Iwo Jima and Okinawa.

According to *Time,* reliable intelligence estimated the number of casualties the American people were being prepared to expect ranged from hundreds of thousands to a million. Feeding in the luck he'd enjoyed so far, he'd calculated the odds on his survival were less than even. Any wonder he'd shouted with joy and clowned in exultation when he'd heard the flat-toned voice on the PA system announce that a device of unprecedented destructive power had been dropped on a Japanese city named Hiroshima?

*   *   *

He clicked off the TV and pushed himself out of his chair. From the corner of his eye he could see Alma looking up from the *Guardian*, toward him.

"I should get some pounds from the ATM. It's my turn. No need for two of us to go out. Finish the newspaper. Just don't tell me a word of what you've read."

Throwing her a quick glance, he saw that she was staring at him quizzically. Unused to practicing little deceptions on her, he lacked the touch to be successful.

"Okay. Though I hate to see you leave the cricket. I have enough cash."

"The truth," he winced inwardly as he uttered the word, "is I can't seem to get into the match. A walk will do me good." So pathetically feeble was his rejoinder that he felt a rush of gratitude for her consideration in ignoring it.

The sky was lowering, the air chill.

After withdrawing two hundred pounds from the ATM outside the bank, directly across from the inn, he started to saunter around the square. His feet carried him through the lychgate of the graveyard beside the parish church at the far end of the village. Immediately inside, on opposite sides of the slate path stood two war memorials, a gritstone obelisk for those who'd died in World War I, a lighter, perhaps limestone, slab for the dead of World War II. On both monoliths were two long columns of names.

So many from a single village cut off before their time, most in their prime. He couldn't estimate the sum he'd get by multiplying the number buried here by a like proportion from all the hamlets, villages, towns, and cities in all the homelands of those who had fought and been killed. And then he thought of the unnumbered who'd died unburied, those swallowed by the sea and those blown to debris or burned to ashes. To say nothing of the countless civilians.

A gray melancholy infiltrated his depression, mist thickening to fog. Beyond the demographic and moral lurked the cultural, anthropological and biological. How feeble the sunlight of civilization in such darkness, how cold and remote the moonlight of art, how rarefied the beams of saintliness! Had not a sudden rage at the silent conspiracy of avoidance, at the hypocrisy, pretense, and self-deception surged through him, he'd have had to weep his grief on the spot.

His feet, about to carry him along the slate path through the mass of gravestones of the village dead, centuries of them, were stopped by the thought of a possibility that darted into his brain as might a fragment of an exploding shell. Here he was, having reached a ripe old age by the merest of chances, sound of body and mind, with a loving and beloved wife, three children, and five grandchildren to carry on his seed, and he'd witnessed and played a part in the murder of the airmen whom, surrendering, he'd seen blown to bits, and in the death of the kamikaze pilot who, trying to kill him, had been obliterated by a five-inch shell. Although he couldn't do the calculus of years and chances, mathematically astronomical as such coincidence had to be, the age he'd approximated for Yuko Miyataka made it possible she could be the daughter of one of the two Japanese airmen. For that matter, she could even be the child of the kamikaze pilot he'd imagined as little more than a boy, who had got a young wife or girlfriend pregnant, perhaps deliberately, with her agreement, as a token of his love and a way to continue his bloodline, before taking off on his sacrificial though futile mission. What of the life none of the three had ever had? Here he was, alive to wonder.

Approaching the parish church, ancient enough, despite obvious extensive renovation, for him to make out traces of Norman architecture, he told himself that in this landscape of tombs and the stones of the past he was clouding his mind with morbidity. As he entered the edifice and slid into a pew near the narthex, an afternoon during a visit to this village in late summer of 2001 came breaking into his mind. Hemmed in by the architectural reminder surrounding him and held by the strength of the memory, he was trapped in a time of no time.

*   *   *

After torching the bed in our room in late afternoon, we stroll the village. We're still simmering, fingers locked, too wedded to separate. With a will of their own, feet take us into the graveyard of the parish church, then usher us through a portal. Damp as a bog inside. Sidling into a pew, we settle rib to rib, to prevent the gloom of the place from seeping between us. Still living in you, my seed will perish there.

Between two massive pillars, the Lady Chapel tells of generations who, laboring for Mary's sake, hewed, lugged, dressed, carved, and piled these stones in cruciform.

A sudden shaft from the sun illuminates the Virgin and Child in glass— sapphire, ruby, emerald, amethyst, gold. Inwardly I vow, two unbelievers, we'll make a sanctum, not of rock by faith, but of ourselves with love.

In the afterglow of passion, the radiance of the jewels of the Madonna obscures the blood that's stigmatized these stones.

A hundred years of carnage across the Channel. Henry's murderous lusts. His daughters' righteous slaughters. Harvests of opium, cotton and slaves. Gifts of Bibles and smallpox.

We breathe in silent harmony until the bells of evensong clang out of tune.

A few weeks later we're back in the U.S., just in time to reprise Babel on a screen. Watch the genius of engineered architecture, twin towers, which prove more vulnerable than caves, crumbling in slow motion. The height of civilization collapsing on itself. A cathedral of modernity settling into a tomb for melted flesh. The slow-motion picture confounds our brain, ties our tongue, and shrivels what we can only call the heart.

No more than it can consecrate those bones and ashes or resurrect the lives I've buried in you, can love make bombs fall skyward, guide missiles to open sea, keep kitchens from turning to ovens for roasting children, bedrooms to burial chambers for brides and grooms, mosques and synagogues and churches to morgues for corpses and dismembered parts of bodies.

There are no sanctuaries for the *sanctum sanctorum* of love.

*   *   *

The clang of the hour brought the present back. Gnawing on his soul was the ache of memory, a spurious relic, born during after-love in this Yorkshire church.

*   *   *

As they were finishing lunch in the dining room of the inn, he tendered a suggestion. No way Alma could know it was against his will, which was overpowered by the grotesque though improbable possibility that had struck him in the graveyard.

"What say we invite the Japanese schoolteacher to have dinner with us this evening? Tomorrow morning she'll be leaving to respect the graves of Charlotte and Emily Brontë." He hoped his echo of her quaint idiom conveyed a kinship he wished to feel, rather than any mockery.

"A lovely idea. Except for our after-dinner coffee with her, she's been alone."

"This time you do the inviting. Since it's for dinner. You know, more formal. And the Japanese have such a sense of propriety."

"You're a bit retrograde, as I suggested before. The fact is Yuko has been traveling without a male to escort or help her. And she's had to be in contact with many men. Besides, she's every bit as easy with you as with me."

"All true. Yet somehow I think she'd be more comfortable if a dinner invitation came from you."

"Meaning you'd be more comfortable."

Not much got past Alma. Though she couldn't possibly know the reason for his reluctance after he'd made the suggestion, she sensed some ambivalence in him.

"Oh, I really don't mind," she conceded in the face of his unyielding silence. "I suppose she's still in Cock's Wold, trying to find the grave of the fellow of infinite jest. See, I remember. Wonder where in Japan she comes from."

"Using some clever discretion maybe you can find out."

"Just idle curiosity. I really know so little about Japan."

Japan. As they climbed the staircase and he moseyed down the hallway to their room behind Alma, the sound echoed in his head like a gong.

* * *

Alma was about to drive to Thyrsk with a woman of the village they'd come to know during their previous visits, to poke around in the secondhand bookshop. He'd begged off, pleading an incipient headache. More deception. Alma had sniffed that out too, though, again, not the reason.

"Come on, Dan, you know you never get headaches. They're all mine. Migraines. And I won't give a single one up to you.

More likely your interest in the cricket match has been rekindled. Or maybe it's just that you prefer not to listen to a couple of jabbering women, the girl thing I haven't had with Yuko."

"You're as right as our government's intelligence is. I want to give you two dames the chance to hatch a conspiracy I'm not privy to. Better check Aurelia's automobile for bugs. I'd love to inform on you to MI6."

No sooner had she closed the door, after holding it open a crack to throw at him, "Ta-ta—hope the headache doesn't hit full force while you're watching cricket," than he sat down at the Queen Anne desk, a centennial piece, he was certain, on the inside wall of the room. On inn stationery he began to write. Struggling to find words, at first he seemed to have to squeeze them out of the tip of the ball-point pen.

Slowly, so gradually he was only vaguely aware it was happening, the words started to flow. Then they were streaming out. In an effort to keep up with what he was reliving as if it were happening for the first time, his handwriting became scarcely legible. Gobs of language were pouring from his brain. As he went on at a breathless pace, his history became the words.

* * *

It's been three days since through binoculars I watched the launch flying the ensign of the Rising Sun pull alongside the *Missouri,* our sister ship. We were anchored so close I was able to see with my naked eye a corps of Japanese diplomats climb the ladder that had been dropped for them, march across the quarterdeck to where General MacArthur, Admiral Nimitz, and a cluster of army and navy brass stood waiting, and salute.

Wearing swallowtail coats and top hats, the Japanese looked so much like a troop of clowns in mock full dress I could scarcely believe that they were the enemy, that I was witnessing a historical drama. As were all those on every ship anchored in Tokyo Bay, all our guns were loaded and primed, just in case. Pearl Harbor had proved that for the Japanese deceit was a cardinal virtue. Apparently they'd abandoned that *modus operandi* and were meekly surrendering.

As the ceremony proceeded, I imagined what lay ahead for the Japanese leaders. It would be no comedy. They'd strung themselves a necklace of atrocities, with which in the name of justice we, the victors, would choke them black.

Crammed with the liberty party I'm part of, one of the first to set foot on Japanese soil after the surrender, the landing craft makes for waterside Yokohama. As I scramble up the remains of a series of docks, I come on stacks of rifles, evidence of total capitulation. Ahead of me there is no city, only devastation and debris. The charred earth is pocked with craters in every direction. As I move away from the waterfront, I see that pieces of tin, wood and cardboard cover the larger craters.

Without the least idea of where I'm heading, I break off from a couple of shipmates and keep walking beyond what I conjecture is the ruin of the center of the city. I'm surprised that I'm only shocked, not afraid. The few Japanese who appear veer off when they see me. It's silent as death. As I go on, the size and material of the debris lead me to believe I'm now passing through a residential section. Suddenly, close to my feet, a piece of tin slides. The skull of a skeleton rises from a crater. Brown wrapping paper covers the face of the skull. Rags hang on the bones.

I guess the ears on the skull have heard my footsteps in the silence of the upper world. Is this assemblage of bones living in that pit alone? I wonder. Might it be the head of a family of skeletons? Down there at this very instant might whatever of strength and breath is left be forsaking another such creature? Might it even be that the one I'm face to face with is inhabiting this grave-home with what already has become its own remains? Hot as the cloudless morning is, I shiver.

The creature confronting me casts the foreshortened shadow of a stickman. All at once I become aware its bony hand is extending a figurine to me, insistently. Hesitating, I make myself accept it, taking care not to touch the proffering claw. While I stand holding the figurine, two petrified fingers form a V. It can't be Churchill's celebrated sign for victory, that's certain. The fingers touch, then move away from bloodless lips. Spreading its five fingers wide, the skeleton raises its other claw, like a policeman stopping traffic. The porcelain figurine feels cool.

I stare at it—a statue of a woman a few inches taller than my hand is long. She's wrapped in a midnight blue robe, with a hood that cowls her head, except for a thick braid of black hair curled on her brow. Gilt-edged and flowing in folds, the robe is brocaded with floral figures—red, orange, yellow, green, brown, all fringed with gold. Lustrous skin is exposed on her toes, peeping beneath the hem of the robe, on her wrists, around the left of which is a gold bracelet, on her hands and fingers, the right clasping a gold scroll, the left lying across her right palm, on her breast, upon which inside a deep décolletage hangs a gold necklace, and on her throat and face. Wing-shaped eyebrows and birdlike pupils are coal black. Consonant with the repose of the woman's hands is the otherworldly serenity in her face.

I'm astonished that a piece of porcelain should survive intact the bombing that has utterly destroyed a city. And I'm stunned that it's been thrust into my hands by hands emerging from a crater dug by a bomb dropped from a plane I may have tallied as it lifted off from, and, if lucky, destruction accomplished, landed back on the flight deck of one of the carriers my ship was protecting.

After gazing with rapt attention and, I hope, evident admiration, I shift my eyes to the eyes in the pits of the skull. They seem no more alive than the eyes of the porcelain woman. Uncertain what this skeleton, who is doubtless exhibiting a, perhaps the only, valuable he still possesses, is asking of me, I smile with all the good will I can project without words, then extend the figurine back to its owner. Instead of accepting it, he points his forefinger at his mouth, and, after returning the V-ed fingers to his lips, draws hard on an imagined cigarette and blows imagined smoke from puckered lips. Again he holds up the five fingers of his other hand.

"Now I get you," I mutter to myself, nodding to acknowledge I've caught on and at the same time shooting up three fingers of my left hand. Still the skeleton holds up five fingers. Tucking my thumb against my palm, I counter by showing him four fingers.

"Ho-geh," comes from the gray lips in a high-pitched voice, more a retch than a moan. I'm surprised this foreign apparition, my vanquished enemy, knows what those two syllables of English mean, can roughly approximate their sound, and has already learned the protocols of trafficking with the conquerors. The realization that what might well be a precious heirloom is being bartered for cigarettes suddenly hits me.

Bending over, I work three packs of Lucky Strikes out of the inside of my left sock, one from inside my right. All are sealed. I don't smoke. Following the lead of my shipmates, I've bought a carton of cigarettes at the canteen in the fantail and stowed inside my socks, for use as illegal tender, six packs, the limit the duty officer inspecting the liberty party of enlisted men mustered on the quarterdeck will pretend not to know I'm concealing. Looting and trading for booty are being winked at.

Hands that form a stone-like begging bowl receive eighty Lucky Strikes in exchange for the figurine. Seconds after the bony torso and skull have descended into their underworld home, the tin scrapes its way across the open top of the crater. As I wander on through the wasteland, feeling less guilt than I know I ought, I can't prevent myself from wondering about the value of my plunder in U.S. dollars.

Noticing some jagged remains of walls off in the distance, I steer myself toward them. It seems I'm on a lane through a suburb, heading out of the city. As I draw close, I can see the walls are yellow brick, unexpected in that to this point I've happened on no brick debris. Across from what's the shattered remains of this building of considerable size, stands a frame house, more like a cottage than a shanty. It looks intact. In front is a waist-high bamboo fence with a gate. Behind the fence, as though prisoners of war, five emaciated human beings, clearly parents and children, are lined up.

As I approach they don't retreat but stare at me silently. The father finally nods. Lifting the front of the jumper of my whites, I slip from the pocket of my bell-bottoms a thin bar of Hershey's milk chocolate, which, also bought at the ship's canteen, I've brought along as a pick-me-up. Over the fence I offer the candy to the father, who, bowing as he accepts it, hands it to the mother. Carefully she tears off the wrapper, breaking the bar into squares two at a time, and gives them to each of the three children. She holds onto the two left over. The way the children devour the chocolate makes me wish I had the power to turn one Hershey's bar into five thousand.

Bending again, I remove one of the two packs of Lucky Strikes that remain in my right sock and hand the cigarettes to the father, who accepts them with another bow. At that instant the terrible irony that resides in the brand name hits me. For three or four seconds I close my eyes, an involuntary expression of gratitude that the man I'm offering the "Luckies" to won't understand. Remembering that I've stowed a book of matches I carried off from the bar of a cocktail lounge named Lou Yee Chai's in Wakiki, when we'd been moored in Pearl Harbor for a few days on our way to the battle zone, I pull it from the pocket of my bell-bottoms. The matchbook had replaced a condom, which I'd used losing my virginity to a prostitute I'd picked up with the matches. She'd told me she was Japanese-Hawaiian.

Seeing the matches, the man breaks open the pack, pounds out a cigarette and offers it to me. When I shake my head, he tenders it to his wife, who also shakes her head. I strike a match, cup my hands over it, and carry the fire to the tip of the cigarette the man is holding between his lips. The formality being observed on both sides gives me the feeling I'm participating in a ceremony.

"I have much gratitude to you," the man says after exhaling a cloud of smoke. His voice is surprisingly deep for so small a body, his accent more British than American.

Astonished at hearing the man's words, I blurt out, "Do you speak English?"

"A little, badly."

"Your pronunciation is fine." Trying not to sound condescending while wondering whether the man would know the word "pronunciation," I translate my compliment. "You speak very well."

The man shakes his head and smiles between deep draws on his cigarette. When he hands the Lucky Strike pack back to me, I hold up my hand and say, "No, no. You please keep it."

The mother, I notice, gives the two remaining squares of the chocolate bar to the youngest, a girl of five or six.

I'm feeling ill at ease. Turning toward the city behind me, I sweep my eyes along the line where the ruin meets the horizon. As I return to the man, I see his face in a cloud of smoke he's just exhaling.

"Very bad," I say. Trying to look and sound somber, sincere and apologetic, I slowly shake my head.

"Americans are so big," the man says quickly. He's no more than five feet three or four, very slight.

"I'm not one of the big ones," I, five feet eight and a well-fed hundred and sixty pounds, reply. "Is Yokohama a very large city?" It's an honest question in that all I know of the place we've destroyed is its name. While waiting for an answer, I realize that to be scrupulous I ought to have used the past tense.

"Well, yes," the man answers. "Very big city."

"Your home has not been damaged."

"Oh no. Very lucky." So he knows the word after all. But he

couldn't possibly comprehend the ironic meaning of "strike." "Many times the bombs are falling near."

"That building across the road, it was large?" I spread my arms wide, then turn my palms in, as if trying to encompass it.

The man nods, blowing smoke.

"Made of bricks." I point to the closest section of the remains of a wall.

Again the man nods.

"Was it a factory?"

The man shakes his head.

"What was it?"

The man hesitates. Then with what seems to me to be obvious reluctance says, "This was school. There I teach students English. But I speak badly. I read more better."

"Was anyone inside? Were children killed when . . ." Coward that I am, I trail off.

"No, no. Children all gone." As I breathe a sigh of relief, he adds, "But many people killed."

"Who? What kind of people?"

The man draws hard on his cigarette, holds the smoke in his lungs for what seems minutes, then slowly lets it out. It's evident he's loath to go on. I try to encourage him by lifting my eyebrows inquisitively.

"Was hospital people. Sick from bombs and fires. Too, doctors and nurses."

"Why was the school . . ." I break off, realizing the question I've begun has an evident answer. "Because more hospitals were needed."

Slowly the man nods. "No more hospitals in Yokohama."

I become aware I'm biting my lip, uncertain whether to prevent myself from crying sorrow or shouting anger. I've no more chocolate to sweeten what can't be sweetened. The man's pinching the stub of his cigarette. Get out of here, I tell myself. As I'm about to say good-bye, the mother speaks to her husband. To me her hoarse voice seems to be chanting. When the man replies sharply, pointing to the ruin of the building, she raises her voice to a shout.

"Forgive, please. She is my wife and cannot know how is the war."

The woman begins to shriek. Her husband jerks up his free hand, palm close to her face. She stops as if her throat had been cut.

"What is she saying?"

The man throws down his cigarette butt, grinds it into the ground with his toe, and stares at it.

"Tell me, please, I want to know."

"She say I must say to you the bombs come during the sunlight. Three times. Many people die." Raising his eyes, he looks directly into mine.

Silence. I close my eyes and drop my head as in prayer, and something between a sigh and a soft whistle escapes me. A scream from the woman makes me open my eyes and snap up my head. As the man slowly nods his head, the woman stops screaming.

"She say I must tell very big red crosses were painted on the roof."

I reach down, extract the remaining pack of Lucky Strikes from my right sock and thrust it into the man's hand. Bowing again, he accepts it.

Without a good-bye I turn and start walking back down the

lane, then strike out across the pitted and debris-strewn land-scape that had been Yokohama, in the direction I think will lead me to the waterfront. I keep altering my course and twice I have to backtrack. There are no vertical landmarks.

While waiting on the shattered dock for the arrival of the landing craft that will ferry the congregating liberty party back to our ship, I survey the devastation along the coastline. I can identify nothing intact enough to serve as functioning shore batteries or antiaircraft installations. Between us and the arma-da anchored in the bay, a dozen or so battered and burned war-ships, some capsized, some half-submerged, remind me of the wrecks of eight battleships and some smaller vessels I'd seen when we lay moored in Pearl Harbor.

All at once a brawny bosun's mate grabs a rifle from the top of a stack and slings it over his shoulder by its leather strap.

"'Tain't loot. No way. Just a souvenir for my boys back home," he drawls in a deep-South voice. "What the fuck, we beat the shit out of the little bastards, didn't we?"

Shoving and pushing hands commence grabbing rifles that are theirs by the ancient right of conquest and sling them over their shoulders. I edge my way in, seize one, and yank it out. It's heavy, a good twelve pounds, I judge, and looks as if its kick would dislocate your shoulder. Certain it's antiquated compared to the nine-pound Garands the marines aboard ship carry, I guess it's modeled on the German Mauser of World War I vintage.

Burdened with what I've plundered, an obsolescent rifle slung over my left shoulder and a porcelain figurine clutched in my left hand, I shuffle into the landing craft, which ferries me across the bay on what appears to be much the same course that carried the Japanese diplomats to sign the document of their surrender. After climbing the ladder affixed to the hull of my ship, I report myself back aboard. The duty officer on the quarterdeck looks the other way as he returns my sloppy salute.

* * *

After reliving his "liberty" (the grotesquerie of the unintentional irony of military nomenclature!) in what had been the city of Yokohama, he felt as though he'd walked across the desolate surface of the moon. Or through the vestibule of Hell.

* * *

When they entered the bar for their before-dinner cocktails, Yuko Miyataka was sitting alone in the inglenook, drinking whatever she'd ordered from the bartender. She looked to be perfectly comfortable with the procedures of the inn. Alma immediately went up to her while he requested two martinis.

"She'd be pleased to," Alma reported as she sat down across the low table from him. "Really, Dan, she's a very sociable person. With poise and self-assurance. You wouldn't have discomposed her, I'm sure."

Contrary to their custom of sipping, he gulped down his martini. Ordered another, for both of them. When he'd finished his second, Alma's was standing on the table beside her still unfinished first drink.

"Alma, what say we have a third this evening?" Occasionally they did what they knew was imprudent—certain to increase his insomnia and leave both of them hung over the next morning. Usually there was a celebratory pretext. Or one of them was feeling depressed. The amount of gin they'd indulge in to elevate their spirits, he well knew, would depress him hours later.

"You have the blahs?"

"Not at all." He wasn't lying, just being deceptive. Again. With Alma. What he did have was quite different and far worse than the blahs. "We're here on a lark to avoid, aren't we? Seems to me to justify a bit of self-indulgence. Since now we know the worst, we might as well live it up."

"You're right. It's worse to be a hypocrite than own up to opting out, going fugitive."

"Would you mind ordering? I want to run back up to the room and change shirts," he explained. This was an outright lie. At the sound of the word "fugitive" he'd winced inwardly. That Alma wasn't aware of the immense difference between the context and significance that prompted her to use the word *hypocrite* and the place where and the force with which it hit him, made him feel cowardly as well as hypocritical. "There's a tab inside the back of the collar of this shirt that's rubbing my neck and annoying the hell out of me. Give me a few minutes. Why not sit with Yuko Miyataka and I'll join you in the dining room? We can drink the third martini at our table. Order soup and fish of the day for me."

To his ear the excuse he'd invented carried little plausibility. Even over a seeming trifle Alma gave him all the ground he asked for.

Once he'd turned the corner of the barroom, he hurried to the stairwell, ascended two steps at a time, and raced down the hallway to their bedroom. Unbuckling his briefcase, he drew out a sheaf of graying pulpy sheets. He hadn't let Alma know that, compelled as he'd recently become to revisit his life during World War II, before they'd taken off for Yorkshire he'd crawled

into the eaves of their home and removed the seven-page history of the ship he'd served on, from the bottom drawer of a
mahogany sea chest that had been in his father's family for generations.

The document was entitled

**DEPARTMENT OF THE NAVY, OFFICE OF NAVAL
RECORDS AND HISTORY, SHIPS' HISTORIES BRANCH**

Stenciled 28 March 1949, it had been compiled and signed by
one Howard Sigler, Officer in Charge, Journalist, USN. Driven
by an urgency to read again—the first and only time had been
more than half a century ago, when he'd begun to write, then
had quickly given up on, a novel tentatively entitled "The Battle
for the Sea of Peace"—a factual account of what he'd participated in, he'd underlined revelatory passages and double-under-
lined those he'd considered definitive. Although rereading had
done nothing for his peace of mind, he'd stashed the mimeo-
graphed typescript in his briefcase the morning they'd left
home, for . . . he really didn't know why.

Thumbing through to locate his markings, he stopped in the
middle of the last paragraph on page four.

> Operations were resumed on 8 June with a <u>final</u> assault
> on Kyushu, but <u>Japanese air strength was so depleted
> that only 29 planes were located and destroyed.</u>

He flipped the page. His eye jumped to the second paragraph.

> Admiral Halsey's Third Fleet carrier forces, <u>now the
> greatest mass of sea power ever assembled,</u> steamed

northward on 1 July <u>to wage a tremendous pre-invasion campaign of destruction against every Japanese facility which could be used for prolonging the war</u>. . . . <u>No attempt was made to conceal the location of the fleet. On the 15th we participated in the bombardment of Muroran, Hokaido,</u> wrecking steel mills and oil facilities in the city. On the 17th, our <u>sixteen-inch guns blasted the Hitachi Mito area on the Honshu coast, northeast of Tokyo.</u> In this bombardment British battleships joined those of our fleet, <u>all units shelling the Japanese homeland at will without opposition.</u>"

The underscored passages ended with

The Yokosuka Naval Base in Tokyo Bay received the carrier planes' attention [a chilling euphemism, he thought] next day and <u>one of two remaining Jap battleships, NAGATO, was placed out of action.</u> On 24 and 25 July the Inland Sea area between the main islands of Honshu, Kyushu and Shikoku was visited with special attention to the Kure Naval Base, where six major fleet units were badly damaged and 258,000 tons of naval shipping were either sunk or put out of action. <u>This was the end of Japanese sea power.</u>"

Up from somewhere in his brain leaped the fact that the destroyer *Callaghan,* the last ship to be sunk by a kamikaze, was hit during the night of July 28, nine days before Little Boy was dropped on Hiroshima. Perhaps this perversely celebratory event had been niched in his memory because *that* July the 28th was his twentieth birthday.

Dropping the pages, he sat with his head in his hands. In his mind he added to the resumé of what he'd been part of, the unimaginable death and destruction dealt to Japanese military personnel and facilities, factories, and cities, with their civilian population, by B-29's, to say nothing of the losses in air and at sea, including planes and airmen suicidally gone.

With their navy and air force destroyed, he asked himself, would a fleet of fishing boats have stood off "the greatest mass of sea power ever assembled," as it bombarded the coast of Japan in preparation for the massive invasion the Japanese knew was coming? Or would the shark-cleaned bones of drowned sailors have grown new flesh, repaired the blasted and burned-out wrecks of their ships lying on the sea bottom and brought them up from the deep to drive off the attacking naval and air forces?

Would the Japanese pilots, five thousand of whom were kamikazes, whose ashes and body parts were scattered, have reassembled and resurrected themselves to re-commit suicide by diving into U.S. naval units? Or, with the supply of able-bodied young men almost depleted, would willing and able young women have climbed into the cockpits of planes that had reconstructed themselves from their own debris and as dedicated kamikazes have wreaked havoc on the naval forces supporting the invasion? Who in what planes would have intercepted and destroyed flock after flock of our fighters and bombers?

Would the millions of corpses rotting in jungles and caves and those devoured by raptors on beaches of the islands that dot the Pacific have come back to life and joined the reported million ground troops and the vast home guard and the hordes composed of civilians, like the skeleton and the little teacher of English, who had survived the bombings of their homes, schools, hospitals, and factories, and armed with the World War I vintage rifles stacked on the battered docks of Yokohama, have driven off the amphibious legions spewed from LST's, LCT's, LCI's, and LSM's, bearing Garands, Browning automatic rifles, and grenades, supported by field guns, howitzers, mortars, armored personnel carriers, and tanks, that were invading their homeland?

Would the untold dead in Yokohama, where his own eyes had witnessed the utter devastation, in Muroran and Mito, whose destruction he'd participated in, to say nothing of Tokyo and Kobe, Osaka, Nagoya, and Sapporo, have produced the necessary armaments and munitions? Were these the components of the mighty fearsome force that would have taken the life of an American soldier, sailor, airman, or marine for every foot of Japanese soil they fought over? Perhaps the Divine Wind, with an unimaginably exponential strength of the typhoons his ship had gone through, would have blasted the attacking planes out of the sky, swamped the approaching naval force, drowning every last man of the invaders, while sparing the sacred soil of those who had summoned it.

Such was the "reality" the military had projected, a reality that compelled and justified the dropping of the first weapon of mass destruction ever used. And the only, except for the second.

With trembling hands, he returned the document to his briefcase. Despite his urge to hurry in order to account for the length of time he'd been gone, he shambled into the dining room where his third martini was waiting for him. As was his wife.

*　*　*

And Yuko Miyataka, who was sitting at their table chatting with Alma. A glass with a couple of fingers of red wine stood in front of her. Untouched martinis were at Alma's place and his.

"Welcome to the gentleman," Yuko Miyataka said, bowing over the table as he sat down across from her.

"Sorry to take so long," he muttered. Then, giving no ear to the conversation in progress, he began slugging down his third martini. Neither woman seemed to care about, or even notice, his aloofness, as he carried on the dialogue with himself.

Oh, the hoax of history! For two generations the myth had persisted, until it had become fact in the mind and conscience of a nation. Reliving at this late date what his eyes had seen, his ears had heard, his hand had done exposed the grand lie. It also had compelled a self-judgment. And now that guilt had been confirmed, finally and convincingly, wasn't he therefore bound, like Dante's sinners, to administer his own punishment? Inter-fused with that still-living past, doubling its horror, was the abomination of the ongoing present, which was blighting what was left of his life.

It was between himself and himself. He wouldn't declare it, even to Alma. Like what lurked behind the black veil of Hawthorne's minister, it was a scene from his life over which a curtain was drawn, concealing complicity, cowardice, shame, and guilt. Was extending his silence all the way to his wife meant to protect and prevent her, a citizen who'd lived through World War II, from having to face a monstrosity? An easy ration-alization. What then was inhibiting him from confiding in and confessing to her he couldn't articulate, except to acknowledge it was everything he despised. He could smell its rottenness, taste it.

And what of the obligation he had to the world at large, to future generations, to the misguided and naïve, and especially to those victims and their descendants who were still alive, one of whom might well be Yuko Miyataka? He couldn't take it on. He was no polemicist, not a trained historian, even though in his head he was correcting and rewriting history. Was just a second-rate writer of fiction. And his story was fact, not fiction. So with his responsibility unmet, he'd have to bear the burden of his knowledge. Himself death's spy and messenger, his conscience unclean, what gave him the right to indict those, some unwittingly, some cynically aware, who were creating a new myth to serve as the history that would justify the devastation of their declared enemies, the slaughter of the innocent, the corruption of the humanity of their own people by dropping bombs and firing missiles of mass destruction?

The loop of the rope on the load he'd have to carry was slung around his neck. The knot might still be tightened.

*   *   *

"So, how did you like Cock's Wold?" he began when a gap in the women's conversation invited him to enter.

"Well, very beautiful village. All stones are light, the color of honey, I read in the guide's book."

"Is it the size of this village?"

"Oh no. So little, no shops. Just pub and houses with gardens. Very beautiful flowers. And the church. Eight sides to its tower. An octave.

"And did you find the grave you went to visit?" Alma put in.

"Oh sure." Yuko Miyataka flashed her smile. "Not big like Scarborough graveyards. Laurence Sterne has grave close against church wall. With much writing on it. Some too hard for me. He was the rectum there. I respected his grave."

"So Sterne was a clergyman?" Alma half-asked, unfazed by Yuko Miyataka's malapropism.

"Oh yes. But I read in the biography the people in the church will turn backs to him when he preaches the sermons sometimes."

"How strange! I wonder why. Did you know that, Dan?"

"No. But I do know *Tristram Shandy* is seriously comic. An anti-novel long before there was such a thing."

Yuko Miyataka clapped her chubby little hands and trilled a laugh. "This gentleman is the scholar."

"Afraid not. Just a hack writer." At Rutgers he'd completed all the course work and passed his generals for a Ph.D. but had never finished his dissertation on Jonathan Edwards' influence on the American Renaissance.

"Hack writer? What is hack? Some kind of writing?"

"Yes, bad writing."

As if her right hand were a fan, Yuko Miyataka touched the tips of all five fingers to her lips, then giggled. "Pornographics?"

"Worse than that. Hack writing is writing no one will buy." He laughed in a way that would let Alma know he wasn't spewing bitterness, just being drolly realistic.

When Yuko Miyataka shook her head, he couldn't decide whether she was indicating she didn't understand or was suggesting he was being modest.

"I know too that Sterne's novel is bawdy. 'Bawdy' means it's pornographic and literary. Which makes it okay. Maybe because he was living in the rectumry while writing it, his parishioners turned their backs on him after they'd read it."

How much of his playfulness was going past Yuko Miyataka he couldn't tell. At least he was letting Alma know he was trying to be agreeable and entertaining. But he wasn't getting on with "it" and time was running out.

They'd had their starter, a crab bisque, and were eating their entrees. Having downed his third martini, he was keeping all three wine glasses filled with a Medoc, which Alma said had been recommended by the headwaiter, who also served as sommelier.

"Please charge everything to my account," he whispered, while Alma was explaining to Yuko that "bawdy" didn't really mean pornographic. Well aware of the looming hours of sleep-lessness and depression, he felt energized at the moment by a welcome buzz.

With Sterne exhausted, Alma had kept things going by throwing questions at Yuko Miyataka about the Brontës. While trying to come up with a verbal primer for starting Yuko Miyataka to pump out what he was driven to have her reveal, he withdrew. All at once she provided him with the handle.

"Has the gentleman ever been to Japan?" As she asked she cocked her head, almost coyly.

"No," he answered without hesitation. Glancing at Alma, he saw she was staring at him for responding to an inconsequential question with another lie that seemed pointless. She knew how come the figurine stood on a shelf in his studio and a Japanese rifle was stored with old furniture in the eaves of their home in a village in Pennsylvania. To allay her fear that he might have sounded abrupt with Yuko Miyataka, he quickly went on. "Do you live in Tokyo?"

"Oh yes. The college which in I am teaching locates itself in Tokyo."

"Have you always lived in that city?" He was trying to make his tone casual, his manner congenial.

"Oh no. Before, I have gone to study in the University of Tokyo. Not the same which I teach. This is very much smaller, with lesser importance. All students are girls. A Christian college."

"Where were you before you went to the University of Tokyo?" He feared he was beginning to sound like a prosecuting attorney, but now that he'd started he couldn't stop himself. "Where did you grow up? Where were you born?"

"In a city on the island of Honshu. Born and grow up."

"Near Tokyo?"

"Well, it takes the speed train one half hour. Fifty kilometers distance."

"Is it inland, west of Tokyo?"

"Oh no. Direction north. Near to the sea."

"What is the name of the city?" It was as if he had her under oath.

"If you have not been the visitor of Japan you would never hear it. It is not very famous. Name of Mito."

He was stunned. Stunned silent. After what seemed minutes, Alma moved things along, innocently staying on the same track.

"Is Mito a very large city, Yuko?"

"A little large but not very. Not like London. Maybe I will say size like York, where I left from train to take the coach to here. Mito could have a little more people."

"Have you been teaching for a long time, many years?" As he took over again, he hoped he was coming off as nothing more than a boorish male, not the Grand Inquisitor putting words in her mouth.

"Well, I would say . . . thirty years. After seven more years I am retired."

"You must have been very young when you began."

"Oh, not very. You see, I married when a young girl. Then too soon my husband died. So at that time I left Mito and have gone to the University of Tokyo. Not many women then."

He knew he ought to slow down and seem less pointedly intense. To ask what her husband had died of would never do. So on sped his brain, recklessly improvising, single-minded as he was.

"I have a friend who was a visiting scholar at the University of Tokyo. In 1966 and '67, I'm quite sure it was. His field was the English novel. Might you have been one of his students? His name was Clayborn Weeks. Does Professor Clayborn Weeks sound at all familiar to you?"

Stealing a quick look at Alma, he saw that again her eyes were fixed on him in wonder. Had she been less self-possessed her mouth would have been hanging open. Clay Weeks was their slightly retarded handyman, who had no more visited Japan than he'd read *Tristram Shandy*.

"Oh no, I regret I must say. You see, I received my graduating degree when I was older student. Twenty-seven years. No Professor Weeks. Then I started to teach."

The gin and wine forced him to calculate with slow deliberateness, as if his mind were a slate and he was chalking numbers on it. She'd begun teaching when she was twenty-seven. She'd been teaching thirty years. So now she was fifty-seven. It was 2003. Two thousand and three minus fifty-seven equaled 1946, the year of her birth. In Mito. Which his ship had been bombarding on July 17, 1945. Beneath the table, he flicked out all his fingers except his left thumb. Nine. Nine months from July 1945 to April 1946.

"I am sorry to hear that your husband died so young," Alma said just as he'd finished his calculation, and she reached over and patted Yuko Miyataka's left wrist, which was lying on the table. So obsessed was he now that when the glint of a diamond on the middle finger of Yuko Miyataka's right hand caught his eye, he thrust Alma's expression of sympathy aside.

"I've been admiring your ring." Another lie. "Is it your birthstone?"

"The gentleman is very kind. It is a ring my mother has given me at her death. What is 'birthstone'?"

Yuko Miyataka's curiosity was an unwitting ally.

"A birthstone is a gem, a precious stone," Alma explained, providing him an opportunity to let up without allowing the conversation to veer off course. "A diamond is one. An emerald, which is green, is another. Whichever month you were born in, the stone connected with that month becomes what we call your birthstone. Many people wear rings with their birthstones in them."

"My birthstone, for example, is a sapphire, which is blue." He hoped uttering still another lie would encourage Yuko Miyataka to reveal what he was after. He kept himself from glancing at Alma. Yuko Miyataka failed to respond. But Alma, who couldn't possibly fathom why what would appear to be small talk was making him so compulsive, came to his rescue.

"If you happened to be born in April, Yuko, your mother's ring would also be your birthstone. The stone for April is a diamond."

Yuko Miyataka clapped her hands and trilled her little laugh.

"Oh yes. It is so. April is the month for my birth. Now I will always remember the birthstone I have." She punctuated her delight with a nod, then held up her ring and touched it with her lips.

"That is a happy coincidence!" Paying no heed to the fact that Yuko Miyataka might not be able to grasp a spoken English word of four syllables, he heard himself shouting confirmation. And he couldn't stop his tongue from uttering more lies, necessary lies.

"Alma and I have a coincidence also—of birthdays. We were born in different months and years. To look at her you would have to believe she is at least ten years younger than I. But I am certain she will not be displeased that I tell you—will you, Alma, my beautifully preserved wife—people cannot believe she is only three years younger than I am. The coincidence is that we were born on the same day of the month. So we can have a double celebration each seventeenth of July, her birthday, and of September, mine. She is ruby, I am sapphire. Might your birthday be the same—the seventeenth of April? That would make a triple coincidence."

Not only was he fabricating, he was spouting nonsense, when cleverness and adroitness were called for, at a speed that gave Alma no opportunity to interrupt with a humorous correction of more lies she didn't know the reason for. He never forgot her birthday, the fourth of February, she his, July twenty-eighth. Although he did know the birthstone for July was ruby, he had no idea what the stone for February was, let alone September.

"Oh no. In Japan, you see, all persons celebrate birthday on the day of the New Year, a great holiday. For month and day we do not care. All birthdays come on one same day."

"But if by chance," he persisted, "you happened to be born on the seventeenth of April, Alma and I could include you in our minds when we celebrate our birthdays. We would be remembering you."

Again Yuko Miyataka made no reply, either because she failed to understand what he was trying to say or she found it absurd.

"What Dan means, Yuko, is that if you happened to be born on the seventeenth of April, that would remind us of the pleasure we've had with you here. Do you know which day of the month you were born on, Yuko?"

While blessing Alma for her help, he couldn't imagine why she was going along with what to her had to be a ridiculous direction for mere table talk.

Yuko Miyataka looked down at her nearly empty plate, as if studying it. At first he thought she was feigning pensiveness, either to be polite or to seem to be playing along with a game she couldn't understand. Then he wondered whether she might be straining to remember a fact that had no significance for her, or perhaps be calculating in order to come up with the day and month of her birth. He'd eaten all he could, not much more than half of the Dover sole on his plate, and was squeezing his hands, their fingers interlocked, beneath the table.

"Oh no," Yuko Miyataka finally sighed. "You cannot celebrate me with you. Twenty-one of April is my born day."

Nine months and four days after he'd spent an anxious night on watch, waiting for return fire from Japanese shore batteries or whatever naval units might be within range, or for a dreaded kamikaze to plunge into the battleship he was on as for hours it bombarded Mito with sixteen-inch shells, each weighing more than a ton. There Yuko Miyataka had been brought into this hellish world. That night no answering fire or planes had come.

He took a large gulp of wine. Feeling tears that swelled in his eyes about to spill over and stream down his cheeks, he feigned a spasm of coughing. While pretending to be catching an explosion of germs that might contaminate Yuko Miyataka, his wife, diners at neighboring tables, he managed to dab his eyes as he covered his mouth with his napkin. A coincidence, far more remote and wrenching than any of the improbable notions he'd begun broodingly entertaining not long after he'd laid eyes on Yuko Miyataka in the inglenook of the bar, was proving to be history.

He might take it as the final judgment, judgment with a vengeance. This middle-aged Japanese schoolteacher, sitting at table with him and his wife in the dining room of an inn in a pastoral village in Yorkshire, must have been conceived close to or at the very time his ship had been bombarding the city her parents were living in. If it had been on that terrible night, when could they have made love, she being the love they'd made? Most likely it had to have been before the first shell had hit. Had it been after, how could they have had the heart? As for during the shelling, inconceivable as it might seem, it was not outside the realm of possibility that while the world the parents lived in was being destroyed and their lives were a hostage to each moment of chance, an egg of fear in the mother was receiving a spurt of woe from the father, and Yuko Miyataka had begun to be. And it could well have happened that at the instant her father had projected his gush of love into the womb of her mother, where its fate was to hit and unite with the target it sought, a shell fired from his American battleship would have blown the lovers to gobs of flesh, shards of bone, splatters of blood, ending the life of Yuko Miyataka before it had begun.

Was there ever a more bitterly ironic drama, not in a play on a stage or in words on paper, but in life? And to think, the Enola Gay had been waiting in the wings.

After he'd won a brisk but polite skirmish about paying Yuko Miyataka's share of the bill, Alma said brightly, "Let's finish our last supper by having coffee and tea in the lounge."

Given that Yuko Miyataka taught in a Christian college, he thought it possible she might catch Alma's allusion.

"Afraid I must ask you to excuse me. Something I've eaten seems not to be agreeing with me." Hearing still another improbable pretext issue from her husband's lips within six hours would let Alma know he wasn't expecting her to believe it. "But don't let me break up the party. You two have your after-dinner coffee and tea together."

Alma, who, he suddenly noticed, had not drunk a measurable amount of her third martini, raised her eyebrows and shook her head just enough to be sure he saw it. Actually, however, not the whole truth and nothing but the truth, but a metaphorical truth was embedded in what she took for total falsification. Although the full force of three martinis and more than a third of a bottle of wine wouldn't hit him until he'd be lying awake in the small hours of the morning, he was experiencing an ache, an ache of sorrow. And afflicting him still more fiercely than his mythical headache earlier in the day or his supposed present indigestion was the pain of rage. Neither the sorrow nor rage was located only in his head or stomach. Commingled, they surged through every part of him—flesh, bone, blood, brain, heart, lungs, stomach, bowels, liver, balls, prick, all of which as one we call the self. Had he also a soul to add to the catalog?

Nor were the ache and pain brought on by the constriction of arteries, a reflux of acid, inflammation, or a pinched nerve. The pathology, rather, was anguish, the anguish of discovering what he'd brought himself to believe was Yuko Miyataka's history, as well as of unwriting, then rewriting history, his history and, he was convinced, while it never would be acknowledged in his lifetime, the true history of the final phase of the war against Japan. In the document he possessed, compiled and distributed by the Department of the Navy, as well as what he himself had seen and done, these interwoven histories had their sanction. What had provided the impetus for his sorrow and fueled the rage that had driven his search and anguished rewriting was that, even while the pain and slaughter and destruction on a massive scale were being perpetrated again, a history that was a fraud was being written and believed. He wouldn't be here to rewrite that.

"So sorry the gentleman is having the disagreeable digestion," said Yuko Miyataka, as they paused in the hallway outside the lounge.

"I suppose you will be leaving on the early coach to York. On your way to pay your respect to the Brontës. I am certain you must know that their father was also a rectum." He used the malapropism not for the fun of it, but to cement the unbreakable though unacknowledged bond that would join him to Yuko Miyataka for life.

"Oh yes. The revered Patrick Brontë. Coach will come at seven o'clock. Sharp." The last word demonstrated her growing proficiency in *l'usage du monde*.

"You two must say your good-byes," Alma put in.

"Well, I thank you too much . . . Dan." The sweetest of smiles appeared on Yuko Miyataka's homely face. He was no longer "the gentleman."

Only half realizing what he was about, he took a step forward, threw his arms around her, and pressed her to him. Her head was on his chest, ear to his heart, as if she were listening to its beat. Yet he could feel her body stiffen.

As he freed her, she stepped back. Dismissing her resistance, he leaned toward her, bowing, and kissed her forehead. Even had her skin been parchment, his lips been coated with ink that was not subject to the fading of time, it wouldn't have been enough, would have been far far from enough.

Before any of the three could utter another word, he turned and went slouching toward the staircase. He hadn't let his eyes meet Yuko's.